Deric Shaw, who lives in Cheshire with his wife, spent the majority of his professional career as a company secretary and accountant. Realising that on retirement he would have an additional eight hours a day to fill he turned his hand to writing mystery stories mainly self-published. He has been writing in this vein for almost 20 years and now seeks approval from a wider audience.

Dedicated to the whomsoever blessed me with
a vivid imagination.

Deric Shaw

A CHANCE ENCOUNTER

And Other Stories

AUSTIN MACAULEY PUBLISHERS™

LONDON • CAMBRIDGE • NEW YORK • SHARJAH

A CIP catalogue record for this title is available from the British Library.

ISBN 9781528902564 (Paperback)
ISBN 9781528915632 (ePub e-book)

www.austinmacauley.com

First Published 2021
Austin Macauley Publishers Ltd®
1 Canada Square
Canary Wharf
London
E14 5AA

To those long-ago teachers and school friends who lend their names unknowingly to one of my stories.

A Chance Encounter

It was my habit at the time, when having worked late, to saunter up to Piccadilly and find a small but welcoming bar in one of the side streets and enjoy the relaxation of two or three drinks whilst mulling over the world's problems before catching the late bus home. On this occasion in one of my favourite watering holes called the Paradise Bar, I was just finishing my second drink whilst contemplating whether or not I should have a third when something occurred that would ultimately change my life in a dramatic fashion although, at the time, it seemed nothing more than an unscheduled meeting of little consequence. As I sat musing to myself, a woman passed by my table dropping her purse as she did so and continuing on her way towards the door. Instinctively stooping to retrieve it, I looked up to find she had stopped, turned and was currently making her way back towards me with a broad, enchanting smile on her countenance. She was certainly very attractive with shoulder length auburn hair, deep green eyes, an oval-shaped face with high cheek bones and full red lips that were currently parted in that enchanting smile. On reaching where I sat, she took the purse that I was holding in my outstretched hand and stood smiling down at me.

"Thank you so much; I almost went out without it. I would really have been in a mess had that happened."

I returned the smile, acknowledging her thanks as I did so, "That's all right. It's easily done. I'm so glad I noticed it so quickly."

It was then she made the first of two invitations that, between them, formed the basis of the lifechanging circumstances already referred to.

"In that case, you must allow me to stand you a drink as a partial reward." The gesture was made as she took the vacant seat at my table placing her purse before her as she did so.

"I'll certainly share a drink with you but only on the understanding that I pay for it. Agreed?"

She nodded and sat quietly watching me as I called over the waiter and ordered our drinks—all the time with that enchanting smile almost a permanent fixture.

For the next hour or so, we sat talking as she told me about herself although, now I think back, only that which she wished me to know. Her name was Rachel De'Vere, and it seemed she worked in the city as a PA to some leading light in the insurance industry. Though she actually lived just outside a small village on the edge of Berkshire, she stayed in London from Monday to Friday in a hotel near Tavistock Square because her boss frequently worked late and insisted, she did likewise. The firm paid the hotel bill so she herself didn't mind although, in fact, she didn't go home every weekend as she sometimes didn't like facing the journey. During the conversation, the one thing she did not voluntarily reveal was her age though I inferred by observation that she would be in her middle thirties or thereabouts.

Our initial meeting led to me asking her out to dinner which she readily accepted. This was followed by us attending an opera at Covent Garden, a Beethoven concert at the Festival Hall, and I even managed to obtain a couple of tickets for the umpteenth performance of *The Mouse Trap*. In fact, we saw quite a lot of each other over the next three weeks or so, but though at the time I attached no importance to it, she would never let me accompany her beyond the foyer of her hotel. Then just as I was beginning to think there was not much point in my pursuing the relationship, she extended the second of the invitations that, between them, would have such a devastating effect upon my life. It happened during what could well have been our last dinner date when she announced that since she hadn't been home for a couple of months, she intended to go down to her house in Berkshire that weekend and would I care to come down as well. My reaction was, I'm afraid, only too predictable, and I suggested we drive down after work on the Friday night. It was then that I really should have sensed something was not quite right as she answered:

"No. My boss is taking his family on a Caribbean cruise next week and wants to tidy up all his business affairs before he leaves which means I'll be working very late on Friday night until God knows what time. Why don't you go down earlier when you've finished work, and I'll follow on when I can?"

As she spoke, she took out from her purse a door key and pushed it across the table along with a slip of paper which, on examination, contained an address along with brief directions.

"Let yourself in and put the key on the hall table. Make yourself comfortable while you wait for me. There's plenty of liquid refreshment in the sitting room drinks cabinet; I'll see you later on."

All this was said accompanied by her usual enchanting smile that seemed at the time to contain so much promise.

My journey down to Berkshire that Friday night was quite a pleasant one. It was an early autumn balmy evening, and I watched the surroundings change from urban sprawl to rich and luxurious countryside as I drove southwards before leaving the main road and following a narrow country road indicated by Rachel's instructions. It was turning dark by the time my headlights picked out an open gateway at the end of the road into which I turned following the long gravel path up to the house, a rather grand three-storey late Georgian edifice which appeared to be set in luxurious landscaped grounds. I wondered, as I alighted from the car, just how such a pile could be supported by even the most generous of PA salaries; surely this alone should have made me at least somewhat suspicious. Unfortunately, a man sufficiently absorbed in the possible future prospects of my pending assignation was far too blinded to such an apparent warning signal. Walking up the stone steps, I unlocked the door and found myself standing in a partially lit, heavily carpeted hallway off which were several doors to a number of downstairs rooms. Placing the door key on the hall table as requested and realising I had plenty of time on my hands before Rachel arrived, I undertook a brief examination of the place out of curiosity.

The door immediately to the right revealed a large study whose walls were almost completely encased in well-stocked bookshelves in addition to which stood a large oak desk with a high-backed leather chair; thick plush Persian carpet covered the floor. Across the hallway, I looked in on a substantial dining room, tastefully furnished with several portraits adorning the surrounding walls. A little further down the hallway was a small but spacious den replete with armchair, small oak table and sideboard on which one or two splendid china ornaments stood. At that point I decided I'd seen enough and made my way towards the end of the hallway where Rachel had informed me was situated the main sitting room. Pushing open the door I turned on the light switch then took several steps inside before suddenly coming to an abrupt halt almost rooted to the spot. There, lying face-down on the fireside rug was the body of a man, the back of his head staved in with the offending bludgeon, a heavy poker, beside him on the floor.

In the years that followed, I had often wondered why, as most others in such a position would have done, I didn't just turn around and leave the house post-haste. Suffice it to say, I did no such thing. Morbidly fascinated by what I saw, I seemed to be almost without control of my movements and, instead, found myself advancing closer to the body on the rug until I stood over it taking in the macabre situation I had encountered. If that were not a sufficient example of risk-taking, I next started to undertake something I had frequently begged television actors I was watching in a similar situation not to do; I stooped down and picked up the heavy brass poker that lay next to the body. Even as I did so, I knew I had committed a cardinal error for someone so obviously compromised, but I was utterly fascinated by the situation and merely stood, holding the weapon and staring down at the massive wound in the man's head around which a great deal of partly congealed blood was visible.

It was at that moment I heard heavy footsteps running down the hallway and turned just as the door was thrown open revealing two uniformed policemen followed by a plainclothes man, I instinctively took to be a detective of sorts.

"Stay there; don't move. I'm detective Inspector Donald Hanley." The plain clothes inspector walked briskly over to where I stood, petrified and still holding the incriminating weapon.

Without more ado, he produced a large plastic bag from his pocket, took the poker from me with his gloved hand before slipping it into the bag.

"How did you get in here; there's no sign of a break in?"

When I told him I had used a key which was now on the hall table, he turned and nodded to one of his constables who made his way back down the hall.

"And where did you obtain the key from?"

I explained I was here by invitation of Rachel De'Vere, and it was she herself who had provided it. Looking down at the body then back at me, he shook his head in disbelief.

"Do you know who that is on the rug before you? It happens to be Sir Philip De'Vere, husband of the woman you insist provided you with a key. He also happens to be chairman of the county council and a wealthy London businessman."

As he spoke, my confused mind started to piece together some of the things I really should have picked up on over the last three weeks: the casual and unlikely nature of our meeting, her refusal to allow me to see her beyond the hotel door not to mention the suggestion that I travel here to her house alone pending her intention to follow later. All this was now clear to me as a perfect if simple set up into which I, obsessed with her as I was, willingly fell, hook, line and sinker. At that moment, the uniformed officer returned, glanced at his superior and shook his head.

"There's no key on the hall table, Sir."

Inspector Hanley turned to me laying a hand on my shoulder as he did so, "I think we'd better continue this discussion down at the station, don't you? Let's get going."

Several months later, I appeared at the Old Bailey charged with the first-degree murder of Sir Philip De'Vere. The evidence against me was such—my fingerprints on the poker handle, illegally present in the house despite my attempt at explanation, no key or other evidence of how I entered the premises—that the jury had little difficulty in finding me guilty unanimously. But perhaps the most painful part of the trial was standing in the dock watching Rachel De'Vere give evidence on oath that she hadn't invited me to her house, indeed that she didn't know me and had never seen me before until that very day.

The Judge, as he was obliged to, passed a mandatory life sentence on me with a recommendation that I serve a period of not less than fifteen years. As it happened, with good behaviour and some clever footwork on the part of my barrister, I actually served ten years in all.

Some weeks after my release and after another fruitless day tramping around the city calling at employment agencies and job centres, I found myself entering the portals of my former favourite watering hole just off Piccadilly in need of a rest as well as some alcoholic stimulation.

The Paradise Bar looked more or less the same as it had done a decade ago on my last visit, and I took a seat at the same table I had occupied on that night. Having ordered and received my drink, I sat reflecting on my life over recent years whilst gazing idly out of the nearby window at the people who were hurrying by in order to catch their bus or tube that would take them home to house and family or those whose intention it was to sample the fleshpots of the evening that London has to offer, when I became conscious of someone having sat down uninvited in the chair across my table. Glancing up, I found myself unexpectedly staring into the face of Rachel De'Vere. A little older perhaps and fuller in the face, she was still, nevertheless, a very handsome woman with her auburn hair tumbling around her shoulders and those eyes like deep green pools that stared unswervingly at me. The only thing missing was the enchanting expansive smile that she'd worn when first we'd met all those years ago. Instead, the face was set in serious, almost stern observation as though she felt, quite correctly as it happened, that any attempt at friendly humour would be instantly rebuffed. I, for my part, was completely stunned into silence as I gazed into the face of the last person on earth I expected to see at that moment.

"I thought I might buy you that drink you so gallantly refused last time." She hesitated for a moment before continuing, "I also thought you might feel entitled to an explanation; am I right?"

During her delivery, the face remained set without the slightest indication of expression. It was clear she'd come on a specific errand and was determined, if allowed, to undertake it personally.

My thoughts were totally confused. On the one hand, I had to admire her bold, almost brazen, confidence given what had occurred between us, whilst on the other hand, I wanted to give her a mouthful of all the pent-up anger and hurt that still festered inside my very being. Somehow, I managed to control such antagonism, instead curiously opting for the chance at last of finding out what had made it necessary in her calculations for me to lose ten years of my freedom.

"The drink I'll accept; as for the explanation, let's hear it, but it better be good."

As the waiter placed the drinks she'd ordered before us, Rachel slowly and deliberately removed her gloves, placed them on the table in front of her before leaning back in her chair, fixing me with those penetrating green eyes then commenced her explanation of the circumstances that had led to my ten-year incarceration a decade ago.

"My husband was a cruel and brutal bastard. I'd met and married him when I was a relatively young, inexperienced woman of barely twenty-three years of age. As a mature man in his early forties, Philip was much more worldly wise with a suave convincing manner as well as being rather handsome into the bargain. This coupled with his considerable wealth and the large house down in Berkshire was more than enough to turn the head of such a young and naïve person as I must have seemed to him at the time. Things were not that bad in the early years. We holidayed abroad quite a lot during which time he plied me with all sorts of presents, jewellery and the like and even had an expensive sports car waiting for me after one such trip so that I felt my life could hardly have been any better. But what I didn't know at the time was that Philip De'Vere had a much darker side to him. As his ardour started to cool, his vile temper started to show, particularly after one of his bouts of heavy drinking. Violence was an inevitable conclusion of these ever-increasing occasions so that I was terrified of even trying to speak to him in case it started a row. Eventually, after having once again picked myself up off the floor as a result of his latest drunken assault, I decided that I'd had enough and made up my mind to leave him. But about that time, I met someone else. He was so different, quiet, considerate and such a pleasant contrast to what I'd grown used to over the last seven or eight years, it was no surprise we fell in love. He asked me to go away with him, but it was then I started to think about everything my husband had put me through so that I became reluctant to just walk away and leave him with everything. His wealth, the house, these were things I began to think were partly mine. Why should I walk away empty handed? Philip was a fervent Catholic, so divorce was out of the question, and I knew he would fight me with everything he had against giving me a red cent. My new lover and I talked about it, and it was after much long and lengthy heart searching that we decided to…"

It was the first time throughout her bitter explanation that she'd faltered in her delivery, and given what she'd told me, I found it hard to imagine it was caused through any sort of guilt complex. It left me unmoved and cynical.

"Kill him; isn't that the phrase you're looking for?"

She bit her lip nodding her head at the same time but never looked away or took her eyes off me.

"And that's where I came into the picture, I take it—the unfortunate, unsuspecting patsy that just happened to be in the wrong place at the wrong time; at least from my point of view."

She was clearly hurt by the bitter cynicism I displayed, but to do her credit she was determined to complete the story and so continued her explanation.

"Yes, that's about it. You weren't singled out; you just happened to be a convenient target when our plan was hatched. That first night in the Paradise Bar, it could have been someone else, but you chose to enter the scene quite unbeknownst and became the chief protagonist in the play. I'm sorry it had to be you but…"

I cut her short.

"Tell me something…why did there have to be a fall guy at all? Why couldn't you just commit the deed and leave it at that? It would have saved me ten years of my life, that's for sure."

Rachel started to appear a little nervous and fumbled with her gloves whilst still keeping her gaze directly on me.

"Because we needed a relatively quick charge and conviction. If matters had dragged on, others would have got involved and awkward questions asked. We had to get the matter completed as quickly as possible to avoid awkward questions arising."

"We? Who the hell's we? I thought the police brought the charges and handled matters."

Her nervousness seemed to increase, causing her to look away and out through a nearby window.

"Did you ever wonder during the trial what happened to the door key you placed on the hall table that night and why the uniformed constable couldn't find it?" She said this still staring out of the window into the crowded street beyond.

"You're damn right I did. That absent key ruined my alibi for entering the house by invitation. What happened to it?"

Her gaze returned to me directly, and her nervousness seemed to leave her as she replied.

"It found its way into the pocket of Detective Inspector Hanley; that's why the constable found nothing on the table when he looked."

It was a moment or two before the full force of what Rachel had said registered and the penny, so to speak, dropped with a resounding thud.

"Jesus! Are you telling me that the inspector on the case is involved in all this? What's more he's your new lover, isn't he? No bloody wonder I was on a hiding to nothing. The evidence had been removed."

We sat staring at one another through what seemed an interminable silence before she answered.

"Yes, that's right. You'll not be surprised to know my name is now plain Mrs Hanley, and my husband is now Detective Chief Inspector Hanley of the Thames Valley Force. A lot can happen in ten years as I'm sure you yourself know already."

I shook my head in partial disbelief.

"And that's it, is it? You inherit a fortune, live in a big mansion with a new husband and I, after ten years' incarceration for something I didn't do, end up on skid row— no job, no prospects and very little future. Nice one, Rachel, I must say."

She sat there silent and stony faced clearly emotionally affected by my response, but how the hell did she expect me to be? Calm and full of forgiving? She'd dealt me a bum hand, and I'd lost heavily. That generates an awful lot of bitterness, and that bitterness came pouring out as I mentally recalled how it all started: the sting, the trial and, oh yes, the intervening ten years staring at a brick wall every day and night wondering just what I'd done to deserve such treatment.

I laid it on with a trowel, so she'd never be under any misunderstanding just how bitter I really felt.

"You realise I could go to the police with all this and have the pair of you arrested and charged?"

For the first time during the evening, she allowed herself a half-smile whilst shaking her head.

"No, you couldn't. They wouldn't believe you, particularly as you sought to incriminate one of their own. As far as they're concerned, the case is closed and the culprit has done his time. I know it's no comfort to you, but I'm truly sorry it had to happen to you; I did like you quite a lot whether you believe me or not." With that she pulled on her gloves and picking up her purse rose from her chair.

"I said when I came in, I wished to buy you a drink as well as give you an explanation. I've done both those things, but there's something else I feel you're entitled to." She hesitated briefly, "Recompense; and I assure you that will be forthcoming before long. Good bye; we won't see each other again, but then I suspect that's something you'll be quite pleased about."

She turned, and I watched her walk calmly through the doorway and out into the busy street where, in moments, she disappeared into the crowds of people passing to and fro along the dampened pavements.

I was deliberating whether to order a final drink or make my way back to my lodgings when Joe the barman came across and placed an envelope on the table in front of me.

"The lady that's just gone out asked me to give you this but only after she'd left; said you'd understand."

I sat with my hand half across the envelope for quite some time almost too afraid to open it in case it contained some further faltering attempt at an excuse for all the pain and injustice she'd caused me. Eventually I overcame my apprehension and slit it open before removing its sole content: a certified cheque from a Swiss bank made out in my name for the sum of £500,000! For a brief moment I tried to reason whether this sum in any way equated with the loss of ten years of my life. I concluded 'probably not' but convinced myself, nevertheless, it must come very close.

A Matter Resolved

The young man reeled in his fishing line before placing it on the floor of the small rowing boat. He glanced at his watch and then up at the sky which, whilst still clear, was showing the first signs of dimness as the last rays of sunshine began to disappear below the horizon. He was several hundred yards out to sea off the coast of Gibraltar and wished to give himself sufficient time to row back to shore before nightfall, particularly, as he noticed a rolling sea mist starting to make its way landwards. James Holroyd was nearing the end of a fortnight's holiday from his pressurised work in the city of London where he was a senior partner in a medium-sized marine insurance company. He'd intentionally chosen a quiet and solitary break in order that he would be emotionally as well as physically refreshed when he recommenced his work the following week. Heaving a sigh as he contemplated how quickly his restful sojourn had passed, the young man reached for the oars and was just about to commence his return journey when he suddenly froze in his seat.

As if brought in by the swirling mist which was now thickening by the minute, he found himself staring at a twin-masted sailing ship which appeared to be fully rigged but remained motionless on the still waters of the Mediterranean.

He knew full well the vessel had not been there a minute ago and wondered just how such a large ship could have suddenly appeared as though from nowhere. His maritime experience told him he was looking at an old-fashioned brigantine, about two or three hundred tons; the sort of ship that was common in the latter half of the nineteenth century and used for transporting cargo around the world. At first, he thought it might have been one of those mock vessels used for giving holidaymakers a nautical experience, but the vessel was too workmanlike and had none of the paint or superficial appearance such a ship would display. Furthermore, as far as he could tell, there was no sign of life or activity aboard. Still frozen in his seat and gripping his oars, James watched transfixed as the incoming sea mist wound around the masts of the stationary vessel and insinuated itself along the deck and over the cabin in almost wraithlike fashion so that the whole scene took on a sinister and eerie appearance.

Although the time that had passed since James had first spotted the ship was but a few minutes, the distance between his own small boat and the sailing ship had narrowed considerably due to drifting so that he was now but a few yards away from the brigantine's hull which seemed to soar above him. Eventually, the boats touched gently, and James reached out so that his hand lay flat against the mystery ship's side, from which position he 'handed' his way along towards its bow until he was underneath the anchor and just where he would expect the ship's name to be. Craning his neck, he peered upwards. At first, it was too indistinct to see, but as the mist parted temporarily, he saw the name clearly embellished on the vessel's side and caught his breath sharply as he read 'Mary Celeste'!

The feeling that immediately gripped him was a combination of excitement and fear with the latter being the predominant influence initially. Everyone in the civilised world would be familiar with that name, and he, who had read extensively about the mystery surrounding the ship, was well-versed in its detail. Even as he sat half-petrified in his rowing boat, the details flashed through his mind like a replayed video. The Mary Celeste had left New York, Staten Island on 7 November 1872 carrying 1,700 barrels of raw alcohol bound for Genoa. On board were the captain, Benjamin Briggs, his wife Sarah and their two-year-old daughter Sophia. In addition, there were seven members of the crew: Albert Richardson, the first mate, Andrew Gilling, second mate, Edward Head, steward and cook, two brothers, Volkert and Boz Lorenson, Arian Martens and Gotlieb Gondeschall; the last four were seamen as well as being German. The ship never reached Genoa. Instead on 4 December, it was found drifting and abandoned just off the coast of Portugal not far from where she appeared now. Many theories of what happened abounded, but even an investigatory court in Gibraltar could not decide with any certainty what occurred.

All this and more flashed through the mind of James Holroyd as he sat in his rowing boat staring up at the most striking name in the annals of seafaring, a name that had passed infamously into the history of nineteenth century sailing. He knew from his reading that the Mary Celeste had, some twelve years or so later, foundered on rocks in the Caribbean in an attempted insurance fraud.

So what was this vessel he sat so close to, he asked himself. A similar named ship that had sailed here by coincidence? No, whatever he was looking at, this was not a present-day vessel; everything about it placed it in the era of the original Mary Celeste.

But what was he to do? Row back to shore and pretend he hadn't seen it? By now the feeling of fear, though not completely gone, had certainly abated while that of excitement had grown considerably. His natural curiosity was taking over so that he now wished to find some way of attempting to board the ship. He recalled that, when found abandoned, only a strong rope was found tied to the ship's stern. Glancing back to see whether it was as recorded, he saw, to his surprise, a rope ladder hanging down amidships; a ladder he was sure was not there when he first spotted the vessel. Guiding his little boat along the vessel's side, he soon reached the ladder and, after fastening his boat to the bottom rung, hauled himself up and started his ascent up the side of the Mary Celeste.

By the time he'd scaled the ladder and hauled himself over the railing, he was partly out of breath and found himself standing on the deck panting. As he stood there, his eyes searched the deserted deck for signs of anything out of place, but as far as he could tell, it conformed to what he had read about the ship when originally boarded by Oliver Deveau, chief mate of the Dei Gratia who first encountered the stranded vessel. After he had regained his normal breathing pattern, James started to walk slowly towards the cabin situated at the centre of the ship, and it was then he noticed something very strange; through the window of the cabin, he saw a dim light as though from a lamp or candle. This, along with the rope ladder he'd just ascended, was yet another departure from the records of the original boarding. Instantly, his mind deduced that something was wrong. *If this was in some way the Mary Celeste, real or imagined, then certain matters, small though they were, differed from the original reported text.*

His hesitation, though, was only momentary. Slowly he recommenced his approach towards the cabin. Descending the few wooden steps that lead down to the door, he pulled it open and stepped inside. The smell was pungent, a combination of dampness, stale tobacco and the aroma of equally stale food. The cabin was in total darkness except for the pale light that glowed from the oil lamp sitting on the table in the middle of the room. James kept his gaze directly on the lamp as he made his way to the right-hand side of the table so he could get a better view of the cabin as his eyes gradually became more accustomed to their surroundings. The cabin was long but narrow and had seating fitted along each side under the windows that would, during daylight, offer adequate light. The walls were wood-panelled with shelves fitted at intervals, and there appeared to be one or two cupboards presumably for storing equipment or clothes. Still breathing heavily, he allowed his gaze to leave the lamp and follow the shape of the room and it was then that he suddenly realised he was not alone! A figure stood on the far side of the room partly hidden by dark shadows, but James sensed its presence instantly.

He was thinking desperately what he should do next when the figure stepped out of the shadows and stood at the opposite side of the table looking straight at his young visitor. "Good evenin' James; I've been expectin' yah for some time."

The words were spoken with a strong American drawl by a man James could tell was from a bygone age, a man he estimated to be in his late thirties or early forties with a shock of black hair beginning to recede from both temples and thick bushy eyebrows. His countenance was firmly set, but the face carried a hint of a smile which, allied to the greeting, gave the young man some reassurance. The man continued:

"Der yer know who I am, James?"

The young man hesitated then, remembering photographs he had seen during his studies, nodded. "Are you Captain Benjamin Briggs?"

It was the man from the past's turn to nod.

"But how do you know my name, and what did you mean when you said, 'I've been expecting you'? You don't know me, and I'm here purely by chance, on holiday."

"Oh, but ah do know who you are, James. You're a professional young man workin' in the marine insurance business in England, and what's more, you've read in some detail what was s'posed to have happened to the Mary Celeste all them years ago; so that makes you an ideal choice for mah 'mediate needs."

The young man retained a perplexed look about his countenance as he tried to work out just what all this was about.

"I still don't understand, Captain Briggs; what am I doing here, and what do you want from me? In fact, is this ship real or am I imagining all this, like a dream?"

The captain's smile broadened slightly as he recognised the young man's confusion.

"For our needs just now mah ship's real enough. Now, yer recall when readin' about what happened there wus all sorts of theories and stuff, don't yer?"

"Yes, I remember. The main one was that you suffered an underwater seaquake which disturbed the stove, and you

28

abandoned ship fearing an explosion due to alcohol fumes escaping."

"That's right, I guess. But there wus no seaquake involved; I can tell yer for sure."

"Some thought you'd been attacked by pirates, didn't they?" James continued.

"So they did young James; but if pirates had taken us, they'd 'ave stripped the vessel bare, and you know from your readin' that didn't 'appen, did it?"

James racked his brain to recall other theories before continuing.

"Then there was the mutiny theory allied to possible drunkenness, wasn't there?"

"That's true enough but do yer think I'd 'ave taken mah wife and two-year-old daughter on a ship whose crew I couldn't fully trust? No, James, there was no mutiny; just as there was no tsunami, no explosion nor no waterspout."

At that point, James, a little frustrated, seemed to lose patience.

"Well, what the hell did happen to make you all abandon ship?"

The sea captain paused for a moment before replying, then indicating his young interlocutor should sit down on the bench behind him while he himself remained standing, leaning forward slightly, his hands lightly set on the table top.

"That's why yer here yerself, James. I figured after all this time, the real facts should be told, and who better to tell 'em to than yerself. So listen good, young James, and hear just what did 'appen to us on the Mary Celeste all them years ago."

Given all that had happened that evening, the young man found it all too difficult to take in his surreal surroundings and accept that a sea captain who'd died some hundred and forty years ago was about to explain a mystery half the world would give its eyeteeth to hear; he nonetheless sat down quietly and listened.

"Ahs yer readin' alluv' told yer, we set sail from Staten Island in New York on the seventh of November 1872 carryin' 1,700 barrels of raw alcohol needed for fortifyin' wine bound for Genoa in Italy. Eight men including mahself was aboard as well as Sarah, mah wife, and little Sophia Matilda, our two-year-old daughter. Things was fine at first; weather fair, a good wind an' a fairly settled sea. Ah spent a good deal of time in mah cabin early on studyin' the charts an' such, so Albert Richardson mah first mate looked after matters on deck mainly just reportin' to me every now an' then, yer understand."

James nodded having taken in the picture of the Mary Celeste's normal and uneventful departure from New York.

"It was when we was two or three days out when things started to go wrong. Richardson came to mah cabin one mornin' an' told me one of the crew was ill. It was one o' them German brothers, he said, the Lorensons; Volkert was his first name. It was him who'd fell ill and mah mate had confined him to his bunk below. At that point, there was nothin' to worry 'bout too much. Illness at sea was common enough an' we can manage usually by the others doublin' up an' such with the work. It was the evenin' of the followin' day when mah mate came to see me again but this time with fear in 'is eyes an' hardly able to speak properly. He said I must come an' see Lorenson but wouldn't tell me why at that moment. It was when I went down to the seaman's bunk an' saw him that I understood mah mate's fear. Lorenson was

30

lyin' on his bunk sweatin' like a pig and groanin' somethin' awful. But what filled me with alarum was his condition. His face was covered in festerin' pustules and spots, an' when I opened his shirt, his body too was covered in them just the same. I was no doctor, James, but straightaway ah knew what ah was lookin' at; the man was in the advanced stages of smallpox. It seemed he'd been on a recent trip to Haiti an' the Caribbean generally and must have contracted the disease there."

At that point, the captain paused as though to allow his young interlocutor a chance to take in the full nature of what he'd been told. It was, in fact, James who prompted him to recommence his tale.

"But what did you do then; it must have been a great shock?"

"Aye lad, it was that. Ah knew at that very moment we would not be goin' on to Genoa. On a small confined ship such as Mary Celeste, the crew an' passengers mix regularly, so ah knew the rest of us was at risk. "

"But your wife and baby, Captain, they were…" James couldn't help interjecting.

The man looked at him with deep sad eyes, nodding slowly as he did so.

"That was the first thing that crossed mah mind, James, you may be sure, but ah had the ship an' all on board to consider. What's more, even if some of us survived the trip, ah couldn't allow such a contaminated vessel to arrive at a major port such as Genoa. Smallpox had been more or less eradicated in the western world; ah couldn't risk bringin' a new epidemic to such a place. Ah knew it was only a matter of time before others went down with the disease, but ah needed time to think an' plan so we moved Lorenson to a separate cabin, told his brother but agreed to keep silent to the others for a day or two. For the time bein', we continued on our original course towards the Azores though ah knew I hadn't much time left before ah decided what must be done. Soon my worst fears became fact when, some twelve days or so out from our original departure, two more went down with the disease. This time it was Arian Martens and mah second mate Andrew Gilling who were confined to their bunks, and two days after that Lorenson died, so we had to bury him at sea. I could keep matters quiet no longer, and after callin' them all together in this very cabin, ah told them the true position and what I was goin' to do.

"Ah recall how everyone in the room fell silent as I explained matters though ah could see terror in their eyes an' almost smell the fear around em' all. Ah told em' we couldn't go on to Genoa an' all I could think of was findin' some quiet deserted place where we could perhaps live out the rest of what was left of our lives without bein' a danger to anyone else. There was protest at first, but ah was the captain an' determined to carry out my plan. Soon enough, they saw there was no other way given our situation. Ah said it was mah intention to sail to the island of Santa Maria in the Azores, a place ah knew to be sufficiently isolated provided we kept to the southwest of the island, and this we did arriving on 25 November."

"I remember, that was the date of the last entry in the log, wasn't it?" James's interruption was acknowledged by a slow nod. "But you made no mention whatsoever of what had taken place."

The captain smiled wanly.

"Does that surprise yer? Ah didn't want any mention of the real reason to come out at that time. Let 'em think what they will, ah thought; we'll be gone soon enough. Anyway, by the time we arrived a couple of miles off Santa Maria, we'd buried Martens and Gilling at sea, and I knew only time would tell when the next of us fell ill. With three of us already gone, it left seven of which one was but a small child, so I ordered the 'yawl', our smallest boat, to be released and readied. We loaded a quantity of food and ah grabbed a couple of instruments before we all climbed down into the 'yawl', and two of the men took oars before guiding us landwards. Ah remember glancin' back at the Mary Celeste an' seein' her just driftin'. It made me sad cos' ah'd never abandoned a ship before."

James made a further observation based on his readings.

"You left your son with your mother back in America, didn't you, Captain?"

Again the man looked sad as he spoke.

"That's right, young James, an' that was probably the most painful part of what I was doin'. Ah wouldn't be writin' or communicatin' in any way in case there was a will to try an' find us; so right then, ah knew ah'd never see either of them again."

A long silence ensued as both parties reflected on what had been said before the captain tried to shake off his lasting sorrow and continue his fascinating tale.

"We landed on the southwest side of Santa Maria in the early mornin' of 26 November, dragging the 'yawl' ashore an' hidin' it behind some bushes near the shore. Then, after a short rest, we struck out northwards keepin' to a rough path that ran higher up but kept parallel to the shore. This was the most deserted part of the island as I knew it from the maps ah read; the only place on this side was Ponta Cabrasante some miles north near the tip so we didn't expect to meet anyone, but that's where we was wrong. After about a mile or so, we saw a figure comin' towards us along the path. At first, we couldn't make him out, but as he got nearer, we saw, to our surprise, it was a monk or priest dressed in a cassock an' the hood thrown back so we could see his face quite clearly. He was quite a young feller with long brownish hair and a fresh ruddy face. He greeted us with a wave and a smile, comin' straight up to us without a qualm. What he made of us ah really don't know; five dishevelled sailors and a young woman with a small child, but as ah say, he greeted us and in a foreign tongue."

"But what did you do, on a strange island and not understanding the language?" James interjected.

"As it happened, James, I'd picked up a few words of Portuguese, so I tried as best ah could communicatin' with the young feller. Then, all of a sudden, realisin' we couldn't speak his tongue, he lapsed into almost perfect English; that was a great relief ah can tell yer."

"And did you tell him about your condition?"

"Yes, James, ah did. Ah thought it only fair to him that we be honest so he could run away if he chose."

"And did he?"

"No. To mah surprise, he just nodded then, beconning us to follow, he started to retrace his steps whence he'd come. We followed him along the path north for about two miles or so before we saw it: a monastery built into a hillside which was approached by a long, steep and windin' path. It was a struggle ah can tell you, James, but somehow, after about an hour's climb, we finally arrived at the gates, then advanced through into a large courtyard where he asked us to wait while he went to speak to his superior. Some minutes later, he returned accompanied by an older man who he introduced as Father Miguel, a large friendly man who greeted us before leading us inside where we all sat down at a long table at which he addressed us. What he had to say, given his knowledge of our condition, merely underlined the genuine sincerity and kindness of these people."

Fascinated by the story he was hearing James prompted the raconteur: "But what did he say, Captain?"

"He said that despite our highly contagious condition, we could stay in the monastery; the only condition was that we would live in a separate wing of the building to which food would be brought to us each day. Furthermore, we would take our exercise in the eastern gardens away from his brethren at least until the final outcome was known. He asked no questions and made no enquiries of our current or past circumstances. Then he spoke at some length to Sergio, the young man who'd brought us, before wishing us well and leavin' us be."

There followed a short silence as both teller and listener reflected on what had been told, the former as though he didn't know how to commence relating what happened thereafter whilst the latter tried desperately in his mind to reconcile what had been said as well as the circumstances in which he found himself. It was James who eventually prompted the captain to complete the story.

"So how did things develop from there—with you and your colleagues, I mean?"

It was then that Captain Briggs, feeling the need to sit down, took his seat opposite his young visitor. He remained silent for some time just clasping his hands and resting them on the table before him. Then, raising his head, he looked straight at James and recommenced relating his story.

"What happened thereafter, young James, was worse than anythin' that had happened so far. Ah knew it was only a matter of time before the rest of us took the disease an' went down with it, but even so, expectin' it an' seein' it happen was two totally different things. The next to go down was mah first mate, Albert Richardson. Mercifully, he went quickly though the disease ravaged his body just the same. Lorenson's brother, Boz, went next in much the same way, then the other German Gondeschall followed. Last of the seaman was the Dane Andrew Gilling who suffered most, lastin' several days before eventually expiring in dreadful pain. Edward Head, our steward and cook, followed soon after. In each case, ah sat with the sufferer an' made sure he had a decent burial out in the monastery graveyard."

A further silence prevailed as both parties sensed the most painful part of the story telling was yet to come, but despite the young man's anxiety to know, he held his counsel until the captain felt he was ready to relate the detail.

"It was on the seventh day after our arrival at the monastery that my dear wife Sarah and our little daughter Sophia, but two years old, both contracted the dreadful disease and first came out in them horrible spots and pustules. Ah had hoped and prayed that somehow, they might be spared such a fate, but that dreadful pestilence showed no mercy as it ate its way through their tortured bodies. Ah find, even now, such difficulty in retellin' what it was like listenin' to mah child scream with pain as mah dear wife Sarah, clearly sufferin' herself, tried to comfort the little mite. Ah could hardly sit an' listen to the noise of such sufferin' an' clapped mah hands to mah ears to try an cut out the screamin' though ah was determined to stay with them both till the end."

At this point, James could see tears start to stream down the captain's face as his trembling hands, held before him, began to shake violently; such was the trauma he felt in recalling the dreadful events that occurred so long ago. It was some minutes before the captain was able to continue, but the young man could tell his host was determined to finish his story for posterity. Eventually, his trauma settled, and sitting back in his seat and in subdued tones, the long-dead sea captain started to relate the final chapter of the terrible events that overtook the Mary Celeste nearly a hundred and forty years ago.

"The end came for both of them three days thereafter on the early mornin' of 8 December 1872. Ah recall foldin' them both gently in the blankets the monks had given us an' carryin' them both out to the graveyard outback. Father Miguel very kindly spoke a few words over their grave before ah gently laid mah wife an' child to rest for the last time. And that, young James, is the true story of what happened to the Mary Celeste and all those on board back in those far-off days almost a century and a half ago. Make of it what you can."

Once again, Captain Briggs lapsed into silence as James was left acutely aware that that was not quite the whole story. He waited a short while in case the storyteller was prepared to volunteer the final chapter but seeing he was not, pressed the point himself.

"But Captain Briggs, what happened to you? Did you follow your wife and child shortly afterwards?"

The captain raised his head and, for the first time, allowed a gentle smile to lighten his countenance.

"No, James. Such are the strange ways of nature and those that may govern from on high; ah escaped the plague unblemished. Instead, ah continued livin' alone in the west wing of the monastery. Ah created a small garden, read a good deal from the books ah was kindly lent and went for long walks durin' which ah often meditated about mah fate and why I mahself hadn't been struck down. Then, after about six months, Father Miguel came to see me. He said that since the disease had obviously spared me, would I care to join him and his brethren and make a life with them. There was no compulsion, you understand; just a kind invitation to become one of them and share their way of life."

"And did you, Captain Briggs?"

The smile slowly left the captain's face before he replied:

"Yes, ah did James. Ah knew ah would never go back home after all that had happened. Mah son would be taken care of by mah mother, and in any case, ah had so much to be thankful for because of the kindness shown by Father Miguel and his brothers towards us all. It seemed the least ah could do was give something' back. Ah worked in the fields with them, had mah meals with them an' even started to learn their language. And just now an' then, though ah wasn't a deeply religious man, ah would find mah way into their little chapel when things was quiet an' just sit thinkin' about mah wife an' child an' all mah colleagues an' what had happened to us since we first set out from Staten Island that fateful day back in '72. An before you ask, young James, ah lived almost another twenty-five years before ah passed on aged sixty-two late in 1897." He paused for a moment before concluding, "Every year ah took as a penance for the guilt ah felt, bein' the only person to survive the dreadful fate that had cursed mah ship."

This time, James Holroyd knew for certain the tale had finished. He sat quietly for a while watching the long-dead sea captain sitting opposite, head bowed silent and expressionless, before he himself rose from his seat. Speaking in quiet tones, he thanked Captain Briggs before turning and making his way out through the cabin door into cool night air.

As he lowered himself into his small rowing boat, James briefly reached out touching the side of the brigantine as if to convince himself something about what had occurred was in some way real though he knew it could not possibly be. As he rowed slowly back towards land, he tried to recall in detail what the sea captain had told him but much of it was already hazy in his mind. And then he asked himself the pertinent question, *What possible use would such information be?* The answer was, of course, none! If he ever tried to relate such a story, he'd become a laughing stock. Everyone knew what had happened to the fateful vessel, didn't they? It had been hit by a seaquake, or was it a water spout, or maybe an explosion or even pirates or maybe... But James knew the answer now. Indeed he was the only man alive who knew exactly what had happened on that ill-fated journey.

He stopped rowing for a moment then glanced back over his shoulder; the Mary Celeste had disappeared just as mysteriously as it had appeared. Only the sea mist remained making its insidious way landwards so that it partly enveloped the young oarsman and his boat as James dragged it safely up onto the shingle and making it fast until next it was needed.

A Voice from The Past

As a young man of barely twenty-eight summers, I found myself in the fortunate position of being able to seek the purchase a property of my own. This had come about due to having received an unexpected legacy from a distant uncle who had recently passed away. As a consequence of this, I consulted a city estate agent in the centre of Manchester with an instruction to seek a property bordering the city but in essence outside it and in the neighbouring countryside. The year was late 1921, and as a broker-member of the Manchester Exchange in Norfolk Street, I was conscious of the necessity to be able to travel daily into the city without too much difficulty. Having left the agent my instructions, I thought little more about it until he contacted me some weeks later and told me he had located a piece of freehold land that was situated in accordance with my wishes, close to Manchester but with pleasant rural views of the Lancashire countryside and already granted building permission. I travelled up a day or two later in order to view the area and pronounced myself satisfied with his choice. An architect was engaged with whom I discussed and agreed specifications and whom I then instructed to commence and oversee building of my future home. In fact, it was the spring of 1923 when I found myself, at last, stood on the front doorstep of my new house watching the last of the house painter's equipment being loaded on a truck and driven away whilst the only other person remaining besides myself, the gardener, commenced trying to turn the surrounding uncultivated area into some sort of acceptable garden.

I had employed Fred Bradbury (Old Fred hereinafter) on the recommendation of a resident of the nearby village of Byford and was pleasantly surprised how quickly and efficiently he staked out the lawns and various flower beds he had planned so that, even before a seed or bulb was planted, I could see the creative intention behind his efforts. All went well during the following three or four weeks as I selected and had delivered the necessary furniture that would turn a newly built house into a home as, at the same time, Old Fred applied his obvious landscaping abilities that would transform a semi-barren half acre of land into a well-stocked rural garden. It was towards the end of the first month, however, I underwent an experience that would change my life in the most dramatic and fearful way.

Having retired to bed as usual late on a Thursday night and enjoyed several hours deep repose, I was awakened suddenly by the most cacophonous noise imaginable causing me to sit bolt upright as I tried to identify the nature of this ear-splitting imposition to my sleep. It seemed to take the form of a loud rattling and grinding of some sort of belt-driven machinery, as though I had been conveyed to an industrial complex that was in full operation. But if such a stark imposition to my solitude initially shocked me, what next occurred sent a shiver of fear through my entire being. All of a sudden and without any prior warning, the most blood curdling shriek of pain rent the air above the noise of machinery that had preceded it so that I sat frozen with terror unable to move a muscle. Then, just as suddenly as it had commenced, the noise ceased and I was left, still upright in my bed, trembling as the beads of sweat trickled down my face. It was quite some considerable time before I could convince myself that there would be no further noise or imposition that night and even longer before I dared attempt to try and sleep. Eventually, however, sheer exhaustion prevailed, and I duly fell into a deep slumber until I was awakened by dawn's early light.

Throughout the following week, I travelled into the city and, as best I could under the circumstances, discharged the obligations of my employment as though nothing concerned me. But in actual fact, my mind and general well-being were in a state of utter confusion as I constantly reminded myself of the strange and frightening circumstances that had occurred at home in the early hours of last Friday morning, wondering what it meant and, more worryingly, whether there would be any repeat of the intrusion in the future. My fears were, as it so happened, only too well founded. At the same time the following Friday morning, I was again rudely awakened by the loud clattering and grinding of machinery followed by that unearthly strident scream of a man's sudden suffering the cause of which I could hardly contemplate.

So distressed and terrified had I become that I didn't even attempt to travel to my place of work that day. Instead, I went down to the kitchen intending to prepare some breakfast, but unable to face eating anything whatsoever, I made a pot of coffee and stood staring out of the window watching Old Fred moving about the garden tending his infant flora and measuring up the next border plot he intended to prepare. Suddenly, gripped with the need of human company, I poured two mugs of coffee and strode out across the garden to where the old man was standing in quiet contemplation. He accepted the offering before we seated ourselves on a nearby garden bench, I'd had made for him, and for the next twenty minutes or so, we engaged in serious but amiable discussion about his plans for the development of the garden with Old Fred occasionally asking my views on his proposed intentions. Such down-to-earth simple verbal intercourse had the necessary effect of calming my shattered nerves so that by the time we'd covered most of his intentions, I felt almost normal once again. It was then, on an impulse, I decided to share with him the events that had tormented me for the last couple of weeks. Not having been able to tell anyone without the fear of ridicule or disbelief on their part, I felt I must share my strange and disturbing experiences with someone who'd at least listen; a sort of unburdening that might just ease my pent-up feelings. Slowly and carefully, I related what had occurred during the early morning of the last two Fridays: the noisy clattering of industrial machinery starting and stopping suddenly without warning followed by the terrifying scream that rent the early morning silence before, itself, fading away.

When I'd finished, Old Fred remained silent for some time staring straight ahead at the house while gripping his mug between both hands. Then, without shifting his glance, he spoke:

"What you eared, Sir, wos the workins' of Norbury's old mill of many years since; an' the scream wos that of poor Jack Stansby as he was chewed up by it. Terrible business, Sir, it wos."

The statement was so short and succinct yet so devastating that I simply stared at him for several moments as I tried to take it in properly.

"What was Norbury's Mill, Fred, and who was Jack Stansby; what on earth happened and when?"

He carried on staring straight ahead and made no attempt to make eye contact with me.

"It 'appened, Sir, back in eighty-four. Yer see, years ago before yer own 'owse was built, there was a weavin' mill 'ere. It was owned by the Norbury family; Sir James Norbury were the boss then an' the mill employed abart eighty people or so, men an' women. The place was full o'shuttles an' looms an' the like, an' when it was fully workin' it made an 'ell of a noise, jus'like yer eared yerself them two nights."

I was getting a little impatient for an explanation of the whole story, so I tried to prompt him.

"Yes, but what happened, Fred; who was Jack Stansby?"

"I'm comin' to that, Sir, if yer please. Jack was the young man who looked after the machinery, not qualified or anythin' yer understan' but kept it oiled an' such. He'd walk along the wooden gantry checkin' things an' lean over ter oil a part now an' then, but one Friday mornin' while leanin' over', ee slipped on the greasy floor an'..." The old man hesitated for a moment as though finding it difficult to recall or recite, "...ee fell 'ead first inter the workin' parts. The scream yer eared sir was the last utterance poor Jack ever made this side o' the grave."

"But that's dreadful; did anyone try to save him?"

"They stopped the machine, but by the time they got 'im art—all them cogs an' belts an' wot not—ee wos a gonner, yer see. Such a mess ee wos that they wouldn't let 'is poor wife see 'im until the undertaker's men 'ad finished cleanin'im up."

The matter-of-fact way Old Fred recounted what must have been a dreadful and macabre accident at the time made the whole thing sound almost surreal. I pressed him for further information.

"You say Jack Stansby had a wife?"

"Ee did sir. A nice young thing called Mary, an' they 'ad two little uns an' all; boys they wos."

"And did the company help or look after her when it happened, Fred?"

His hands seemed to tighten around the mug he held as he grunted angrily.

"The only 'elp poor Mary an' her kids got was out on ter the street when the bailiffs came. It were a tied cottage yer'see, Sir, an wiv Jack gone, they moved in another man an' is fam'ly wivin a week."

"Good God, man; how could they do such a thing? What happened to the poor woman?"

Old Fred seemed to relax slightly from his previously tenseness before placing his mug on a nearby table.

"She spent some time at one o'them missions run by the church in Manchester before movin'out ter Chadderton where she were workin' in service somewhere in return for board and keep. Arter that, Sir, God only knows what 'appened to her an' the bairns, bearin'in mine' it were nearly forty year ago when it 'appened."

"Did anyone…"

But Fred decided at that point he didn't wish to continue the conversation. Standing up, he muttered something about 'getting on wiv'me work' before disappearing into his garden

46

shed. I respected his wishes and returned to the house. I did not speak again to Fred about the matter, but in the early hours of the following Friday morning, there was a conversation from an unexpected source that not only enlightened me about the accident but also left me numb with fear and apprehension.

Being aware of what was going to happen, I decided to remain awake, sat up in bed rather than, as previously, asleep before being noisily awakened in the early hours.

As in the past, the dreadful clattering of machinery started before that excruciating scream of pain pierced the air and flooded my head despite having clasped my hands to my ears. When it eventually ceased, I readied myself to lie down and try to get some sleep but then, I saw it!

Right opposite my bed, between the window and the door, was an alcove across which I had draped a simple curtain until I decided what to do with it. There was a moon that night and it threw a pale eerie light through the window on to the alcove so that I saw, through the thin curtain, the shadow of a human figure. Just the head and shoulders were outlined, and they moved slightly and occasionally from side to side as though agitated in some way. Fear held me rigid as I watched the shadowy figure move about though it made no attempt to emerge or reveal itself. Terrified, I just sat bolt upright watching and wondering what would happen next.

It was then that the apparition, for that's what I felt certain it was, addressed me in subdued almost garbled tones so that I could barely make out what it said.

"Your wonderin' who it is tharts disturbin' your peace at such an ower arn't yer, young Sir. Well, I'm Jack Stansby an' yer knows all abart'me now, don't yer, young Sir, from

Ole'Fred, your gardner. Ole' Fred's a good man, he is, an' ee was there when it 'appened all them years ago now, but ee doesn't know wart I'm wantin' from you now, does ee, so I've come misen'ter tell yer."

The garbled voice ceased at that point, and though I was still petrified, I felt in some way I must try and communicate with the spectre and find out just what this was all about. I managed to stammer out an enquiry to this effect.

"What is it you want from me, Jack? What can I possibly do for you now that your…" I hesitated in fear of saying the wrong thing and upsetting him.

"Now that I'm dead, yer mean. Don't be shy, young Sir; its bin' thart way for a long time now, don't yer see. Anyway, yer arsk wot yer can do fer me now; well, I'll tell yer just wot yer can do. Yer can get justice for my poor Mary, that's wot'. She wos treated badly by them at Norbury's when I got killed an' they've done nowt for 'er since either. She's worked an' struggled all 'er life, forty year or more, brought up two bairns by washin' an' cleanin' for others an' gettin' next to nowt' in return, so I warnts yer, young Sir, to get 'er some compensation an' make them bastards at Norbury's pay fer it. That's wot I warnt yer ter do, an' I'm eer ter see yer does it."

As he spoke, the shadow behind the curtain moved uneasily from side to side as though in nervous agitation, but its voice had made its point clear enough. In desperation, I tried again to reason with it.

"But Jack, why me? I had nothing to do with your dreadful accident, and I have no influence in the matter. Besides, it was a long time ago and…"

"Yer'll do as I say, young Sir, or else it'll be the worse for yer, I promise. My Mary's worked 'erself almost ter death an' is still workin' cleanin' fer others at turn' sixty. That's not right nah, is it? So lissen ter wot I say. Yer works in the city, yer does. Find them wot knows 'appened an' start gettin' justice for my Mary as she deserves. If yer does thart, I'll leave yer in peace, but if yer don't, then I'll go on visitin' yer fer the rest of yer miserable life an' the noise an' screams'll keep 'appenin until one nite, one nite I'll come art from be'ind this curtain an' then, young Sir, ah don't need ter tell yer wot yer'll see cos Ole'Fred made it plain enough when yer spoke now, didn' ee? Wot's left o'me arter they pulled me art o'them wheels an' cogs thart day forty year ago aint somethin' no 'uman bein' should ever be' old. So be warned, young Sir, I'll be gone now, but mine' wot I've tole yer; I won't be far away, yer can lay ter thart."

I sat stiff and upright in terror as slowly the apparition faded until the moon played its pale light on what was now just an empty alcove with a semi-transparent curtain over it. But though the sight of that weird silhouette moving sinisterly from side to side had gone from my sight, it remained deeply embedded in my inner thoughts so that my attempts to sleep were, that night, futile. It was a tired and emotionally drained young man that rose from his bed later that morning in preparation for the daily journey into Manchester and the day's demands of the Exchange—an obligation which, somehow, I managed to discharge albeit with the greatest difficulty.

Several days later, I found myself sitting opposite a solicitor friend of mine in his office in Spring Gardens, a short distance from Norfolk Street and the Exchange. I had telephoned him with a request a couple of days previously, without revealing my personal interest, asking that he seek out what information he could about an accident that occurred at Norbury's Mill some forty years ago in 1884.

"You asked me to turn up details of what happened at Norbury's Mill all those years ago when a man called Jack Stansby was killed in an accident." I nodded. "I assume, through your request, that you are already familiar with the fatality itself and how it occurred?" Again I affirmed my agreement. "Well, it seems that at the time because the widow, Mary Stansby, had no financial resource, the union that represented the weavers in the mill offered to support her in the matter so that there was, initially, an action for negligence drafted and tentatively submitted. However, before it was lodged in the court listings, it was withdrawn and the matter dropped."

"Oh, why was that then?"

He shrugged his shoulders.

"It could have been for a number of reasons: lack of evidence, no witnesses or…" he hesitated.

"Or what exactly?" I asked.

"Maybe there was pressure from somewhere inside the company; it wasn't or isn't, for that matter, entirely unknown, you know. Anyway, for whatever reason, the intended action was withdrawn."

I cursed under my breath.

"And poor Mary Stansby ended up penniless, fending for herself and two children alone."

He looked at me enquiringly.

"What's your interest in such an outdated event anyway?"

I ignored the question and pressed on with my enquiries.

"Tell me; is the company still in existence?"

"Oh yes; they actually pulled down the old mill in 1902 but moved and built a new one near Chadderton so the company's entity continued. There was no break in its existence."

"Which means," I further enquired, "that any liability beforehand would still remain to this day?"

His look of enquiry deepened.

"If there had been proven liability, yes, it would travel over time. But what's this all about; it was all so long ago?"

Again I avoided directly his inquisitiveness.

"And if, hypothetically of course, someone wished to reinstate such an action, what specifically would they need to do, I mean in terms of evidence or witnesses and such?"

He smiled broadly.

"Hypothetically, of course. Well, firstly, he would need to contact the plaintiff Mary Stansby and persuade her to agree to sue the company, assuming, of course, she was still alive and contactable. Then he would need witnesses."

"And were there any witnesses listed in the original intended action?"

"Yes indeed. But first you…" he smiled and corrected himself, "He needs to know the basis of the action. You see, Jack Stansby's job was to walk the gantry and, where required, apply lubrication to the moving parts. Now there was a metal guard to each machine with a small window for access, but in order to speed up the operation, it was often left off and this, unfortunately, caused the fatality. It was alleged in the action that Jack Stansby and his assistant Bill Tennant complained to the management several times about the guard being left off, but nothing was ever done. So Bill Tennant would have to be found and asked to verify this then appear as a witness in court."

"I see. And is anyone else involved; any further witnesses?"

"Just one. It was further alleged the request for action was communicated to the foreman, one Roland Fletcher, but even if you find him, he might prove to be difficult to persuade being a long-serving company man. But he would be seen as an agent of the company, and if complicit, this would be damning evidence against them. It goes without saying, of course, that these people, if still alive, will all be long retired."

I remained silent for a while before posing one further question.

"Is there anything else required before I tell the interested party?"

He smiled.

"Just the small matter of finance. We solicitors', not to mention the barrister, are not completely altruistic, you know. Besides, given the likely damages if successful, I suspect this case may be strongly defended and time-consuming."

I nodded as I rose from my chair. My legacy was more than sufficient to withstand the costs I felt despite buying the house. Besides, given the threat I had received from Jack Stansby's apparition, there wasn't much else I could do.

Having arranged to take some leave from my employment, I commenced setting about finding the parties whom the solicitor had mentioned, with the widow, Mary Stansby, being first as, without her, the action could not be revived. As it happened, she proved relatively easy to find due to her having remained close to the area she had occupied in her early days. I knocked on the door of a small terraced house, the end one in a row of five, just on the outskirts of Oldham. It was opened by a small frail-looking woman with grey hair, a lean narrow face but nonetheless, a kindly smile. Though more than a little surprised when I introduced myself and told her what I intended, she received me politely and listened intently to what I had to say, after which she agreed, albeit a little tentatively, to lend her name to the proposed action. No doubt she felt that, given the stressful life she had endured, assistance of any sort, no matter how belated, would be welcome. I myself was surprised and a little relieved that she did not query why matters had been re-visited, a question which, if had it been posed, might have caused me some embarrassment.

Bill Tennant's whereabouts proved a little more difficult, but I eventually contacted him in the South Manchester suburb of Burnage. He too received me politely and was more than willing to appear as a witness if it proved to be of assistance to his late colleague's widow. He also confirmed that he and Jack Stansby had, more than once, spoken to the foreman about the restoration of machine guards and were told this request would be communicated to the works manager, but of course, nothing was done until after the accident occurred. Latterly, it was necessary to locate Roland Fletcher, the foreman, in an attempt to secure the testimony that would complete the line of responsibility of Norbury's and condemn their lack of action prior to the fatality. He had retired some years ago to a comfortable residence in the suburbs of Weaste near the city of Salford. On my arrival and introduction, he appeared polite but wary then listened without interruption to what I had to say. Alas, his eventual reaction was much as the solicitor had warned me about, making it clear he was not prepared to support the action or testify as a witness as his current circumstances were supported by a modest but adequate pension provided by his former employer who he felt would probably withdraw the support if he did so. Despite my fervent pleas on behalf of poor Mary Stansby, he remained apologetic but adamant in his refusal. I drove back home feeling more than a little despondent knowing that without the foreman's testimony, the action might fail through lack of firm evidence as it would then be a question of Bill Tennant's word against the company. The following day, I nevertheless returned to the office of my solicitor friend and gave instructions to commence the action. We would have to take our chance on the jury believing our evidence although I remained inwardly terrified of the likely consequences if they did not.

The legal proceedings commenced at the High Court in Manchester in early November, and it soon became apparent that with the financial and political influence the company wielded, it was going to be a difficult task persuading a jury of the justice in our case. Certainly the testimony of the plaintiff, Mary Stansby, covering the deprivation and worry she suffered played in our favour as did the company's callous attitude to her and her children after the accident, but nevertheless, defending counsel seemed to have sown sufficient seeds of uncertainty that the evidence of Bill Tennant might not prove adequate on its own.

As was my habit now, I sat upright and awake in bed that Thursday night awaiting the imposition of my weekly torment that had become such a miserably integral part of my life. Sure enough, in the early hours of Friday morning, the manic cacophony accompanied by the piercing scream of pending death rent the air as I covered my ears to no avail though my eyes were firmly set on the curtained alcove which was clearly outlined by the pale moonlight entering via my bedroom window and inside which soon appeared the outline of my threatened nemesis in the form of Jack Stansby's apparition.

"Things aint goin' well fer us, are they, young Sir?" The spectral visitor was clearly appraised of what occurred in the courtroom. "Somethin's got ter change if my Mary's goin'ter get 'er just desserts now, aint it?"

I tried to think of something convincing to say that might allay his fears of imminent failure, but so rigid with terror was I that I could merely mumble some incoherent half explanation which he sharply dismissed. When he spoke again, it was slowly and with menace.

"Ah don't care nothin' for yer lame excuses, young Sir. Yer better listen to wot ah say an' see it 'appens. Yer gotta get justice fer my Mary or else ah'l giv'yer such a shockin' vision that yerl never 'av'annuver sane thought in yer 'ead ever again. They'll take yer ter the asylum screamin' an' cryin' fer mercy, an' I'll stalk yer nights fer't rest o'yer nat'ral life ah will. Yer'll neer know when ah'm comin' or where it'll be so yer life'll be one neer'endin torment so it will."

As I sat frozen in mortal fear, he hesitated for a moment before completing his threat.

"Everythin' ah say ah means, young Sir. Get justice fer my Mary an' yer'l be free of me an' the noise… Fail an' yer knows wot ter expect."

With that final warning, he was gone, but I was in no doubt that any failure on my part and I would never rid myself of this perpetual torment.

I spent a desperately disturbed and sleepless night and rose the following day convinced that if I did not achieve the desired objectives of Jack Stansby's apparition, my life would become a long and terrible torment from which it would be impossible to escape. I made up my mind to effect one last desperate throw of the dice; I must approach Roland Fletcher, the retired foreman, once again in an effort to persuade him to testify on our behalf. Without his testimony, Mary Stansby's action for negligence would almost certainly fail, and with that failure, I myself would be condemned to a life of fear, misery and torment—something I very much doubted that I could survive for very long.

So it was that the following afternoon, after the court proceedings had concluded for the day, I drove steadily and with determination through the streets of Salford towards the area of Weaste that I visited when first I had spoken to Roland Fletcher. It was late afternoon and already going dark, so visibility was somewhat restricted causing me to exercise the caution of driving slowly. As I travelled along, I became aware of a young boy running along the pavement just ahead. He would, I surmised, be about ten or eleven years old with a school satchel slung over one shoulder. As he ran, something in his movements told me he was going to change direction, causing me to slowly commence braking as a further precaution. Suddenly, he turned and, without warning or indication, started to run across the road at which point I braked, bringing the car to a sudden halt. He ran across my path, but as he did so, a truck that had been following decided to overtake my car and struck him sending him rolling into the gutter where he lay seemingly motionless.

Instinctively, I quickly crossed the road and, kneeling over, felt his pulse. He was, mercifully, still breathing though blood was running out of one side of his mouth and also from cuts on his legs. Gently picking him up, I took him back to my car. As I crossed the road, I shouted to the truck driver, sat petrified in his cab, to contact the police and tell them I was taking the boy to Salford Royal Hospital near Adelphi. Placing the young fellow in my passenger seat beside me, I turned the car around and made my way back to the city as fast as I safely could.

By the time I pulled up outside the hospital, it was completely dark except for one or two dimly lit street lights nearby that threw a subdued lighting over the front of the hospital. Rushing around the car, I lifted the boy gently from the passenger seat, mounted the stone steps and pushed my way through the double swing doors where I found myself in a long, wide passageway, well-lit and very busy with staff and visitors moving about in all directions. As luck would have it, a staff nurse nearby saw my plight and, in a moment, summoned a fellow nurse who then helped place the young boy on a wheeled stretcher and supervised his removal to an emergency area leaving me stood, but relieved, watching patient and carers disappear through distant corridor doors.

When I recovered my composure, I approached the reception desk and told my story including the fact I had asked the truck driver to inform the police as well as admitting I had no idea who the young boy was or where he lived. The reception nurse smiled her understanding then suggested I sat on a nearby bench and waited until someone returned with news of the boy's progress. It was more than an hour later when the staff nurse returned.

"The boy is poorly but out of danger thanks to your prompt action. Would you care to sit with him for a while? He's in ward seven on the next floor."

Moments later, I found myself entering a small side ward in which the only occupant was the young boy himself. Heavily bandaged, with intravenous drip tubes in his arm, he looked a frail, pathetic lost soul very much in need of the care and love of his parents whom I hoped had been notified by now. I placed a chair close to his bed and sat watching him as the inhalant mask moved in and out in response to his gentle breathing, a sign I optimistically took to be an indication of his continued recovery.

It was probably a combination of the stressful day in court, the effect of the accident itself and the almost total lack of sleep the previous night that caused me to become drowsy and eventually lose consciousness. I don't know how long I slept, but when I eventually awoke, the first thing of which I became aware was that there were others present in the ward. As my gaze focused in the dimly lit room, I saw, sitting opposite on the other side of the boy's bed, a man and woman whom I took to be his parents. As I looked across, they smiled and nodded, a sign that they had been told of my involvement in the matter. There was also another figure in the room, a man it seemed but sat further back in the shadows so his person could not clearly be discerned. As the boy's parents were now in attendance, I decided it was time I left and rising from my chair made my way towards the door, noticing as I did so from the corner of my eye the man in the shadows leave his seat and follow me. Once out into the corridor, I felt a restraining hand on my shoulder and turning found myself looking directly into the face of Roland Fletcher, the retired foreman from Norbury's Mill.

"I wanted ter thank yer for what yer did."

I looked at him somewhat confused.

"The young boy in there, he's me grandson. The sister told me what yer did, actin' so quickly an' savin' his life. I don't know what I'd 'ave done if he'd died. Yer see, ee's all I've got now me wife's died. So as I've said, I can't thank yer enough."

I nodded and was about to turn away seeing as I was tired and wanted to get home as soon as I could, but he held my arm and continued talking nervously.

"I can never repay yer for what yer did, Sir, but I can help in yer legal case. Tell yer lawyer I'll testify on bealf' of Mary Stansby against Norbury's. It'll probably cost me mi'pension, but it's the least I can do for what yer did terday. Tell yer brief, Jack Stansby an' his mate Bill Tennant both came ter me over the metal guards moreun'once, but when I told the works manager, he wouldn't listen; said things worked better without 'em."

I took his hand and shook it warmly with a feeling of great relief then made my way down the corridor with a spring in my step I hadn't experienced for many a long day. All the way home, I felt so light-hearted as though a great weight had been lifted from my shoulders.

Roland Fletcher was as good as his word. Later that week, he stood in the witness box and gave his evidence boldly and clearly while Sir James Norbury, the fourth generation thereof, sat scowling in the well of the court. It was enough to convince the jury who brought in a unanimous verdict in favour of the plaintiff, Mary Stansby, who, herself, sat in total confusion as to what went on around her. After some deliberation, the presiding judge awarded her damages of £150,000 for the loss of her husband plus an additional £50,000 exemplary damages for the cynical and peremptory treatment she had received at the hands of the company after the accident. Mary Stansby would no longer be obliged to take in other people's washing in order to survive. In the corridor outside the court, she approached me as I waited to speak to our barrister.

"I never asked yer why yer got involved in all this cos yer weren't part of it really, was yer'?

I didn't know what to say; I'd dreaded her asking this question right from the start. Then she gave me a smile and a look of deep understanding.

"It were Jack, weren't it? Ee come ter'see yer, I'll bet. It's jus' the sort o'thing our Jack'd do, I'll be bound. Jus' so I'd get some 'elp after all this time. Thank yer, Sir, anyway. God bless yer for wot yer done." She squeezed my arm before turning and walking away towards the staircase.

Jack Stansby kept his word also. Although I sat up that Thursday night in half-expectancy of another visit, the following morning nothing happened. In fact, I never had any further interruption or experience from that day to this. There was one strange thing though; Old Fred the gardener disappeared. There was no notice or message; he just never appeared at the house again. I never really understood why. Was it something to do with the job? Or maybe, now that Jack and Mary Stansby had at last settled their difficulties, he felt he ought to depart the scene as well. Who knows?

All that was a long time ago. Now I'm a mature family man with a wife and two children worrying what to make of the war clouds currently gathering over Europe and its disputing adversaries. But sometimes when I sit alone in my study looking out onto the now fully mature front garden, the fruit of Old Fred's early labours, I think of what happened all those years ago when, one night, I was abruptly awakened from my slumbers by a cacophonous rattle of belted machinery accompanied by the most heart-rending scream of pain which propelled me into the past life of a dreadful fatality forty years before.

Flying Saviour

The young man kicked his holdall a few feet further along the floor as the queue he was standing in at the airport moved a little further towards the security check-in desk. He was feeling relaxed and content having just finished a fortnight's holiday in sunny Barcelona and felt fit and ready to start his newly acquired job at one of London's more prestigious insurance companies on the following Monday. Glancing at his watch, he estimated that, should there be no serious delay, he would be home before 9 pm that night. Barely twenty years of age, Alan Townsend still lived at home and felt sure his mother would have his favourite meal in the oven waiting for his return. He was lucky really, he thought. Given the state of the economy and the shortage of jobs, he had done well to secure the position he would start next week, and the fact that he still lived at home meant he was not locked into or struggling to enter the property market in its current unpredictable state. All in all, he was, as things stood, a content and satisfied young man who expected to remain in such a satisfactory state of existence for quite a few more years before seeking to change his style of living.

Sometime later, he mounted the metal staircase leading up into the aircraft and, after showing the stewardess his boarding card, soon found his seat some four rows from the front. Pushing his holdall under the seat in front, he settled down for what should be a comfortable two-and-a-half-hours flight back to Heathrow where he would get a taxi and be home by the allotted time. He fastened his seatbelt and watched casually as the usual safety instructions were gone through while the plane taxied towards its take-off slot on the runway before the pilot opened the throttle and made the engines roar preparatory to take-off. The plane surged forward picking up speed before its nose lifted and the aircraft soared upwards heading due westward. Alan had been allotted a seat on the aisle which enabled him to leave if necessary without disturbing other passengers. As the plane settled down on an even course, he decided to try and get some sleep to compensate him for the early start that morning which, otherwise, might catch up with him the following day. Closing his eyes, he soon dozed off, helped by the throb of the engine, and remained asleep until he felt a slight squeeze of his arm and a woman's voice brought him back to his senses.

"Excuse me, Sir. I'm sorry to disturb you."

It took a moment or two before he returned fully to consciousness, and when he did, he looked up to see the face of a stewardess smiling down at him. She seemed a little older than the rest of her colleagues, he thought, but she was still a handsome-looking woman with a pleasant smile.

"Yes, what is it?" he belatedly responded.

The woman was kindly apologetic.

"The pilot has received notice that we may have some turbulence shortly, and I wondered whether you might like to move nearer the back of the aircraft. It's sometimes not so bad there. I have a seat on the aisle just like this one."

Smiling in return, Alan thanked her and was about to refuse, saying he wasn't at all nervous flying, when he felt her hand press a little firmer on his shoulder and he noticed what he took to be a more serious look appear briefly on her face.

"The turbulence isn't quite as noticeable when you're sitting near the rear of the plane."

The woman remained softly spoken but nevertheless, quietly insistent. Not wishing to offend someone who had shown such consideration, he nodded, picked up his holdall and followed her back down the aisle towards the rear of the plane, stopping four rows from the rear where she guided him into the vacant aisle seat.

"Thank you miss…?"

The woman pointed to her identity badge

"Eleanor. Eleanor Swift, in fact. Are you comfortable? Let me know if you need anything further. I'll let you get on with your little nap."

Alan smiled and nodded his thanks watching her as she made her way back towards the front before disappearing behind the plastic curtain into the kitchen. As he fastened his safety belt, he couldn't help thinking that there was something about the kindly stewardess, something unusual but also something he couldn't quite put his finger on. Leaning back in his seat, Alan soon drifted off once again, but when he awoke the next time, it wasn't to the gentle touch of a stewardess's hand but the buffeting of the aircraft as it fought the wind and lashing rain that assailed it. For a moment, Alan was startled; then he remembered the words of the friendly air hostess and why he now found himself at the rear of the plane. At that moment, the pilot's voice came over the intercom. It was clearly an effort to reassure his passengers.

"I'm afraid we're moving into a short period of turbulence, ladies and gentlemen, but we're not far from the channel now so we should be in London shortly. I'll keep you informed as we approach landing."

The storm was fierce and seemed to be getting worse. Alan saw bright flashes of lightening from time to time which lit up the sky and outlined the wings of the plane momentarily before all went dark again. The plane was taking a heavy buffeting which caused some people on board to huddle together in a quiet state of apprehension. Most of them had flown many times before but few had experienced anything as turbulent as this. Once again, the pilot's voice came over the airwaves.

"We'll be making our descent to Heathrow shortly, ladies and gentlemen. Make sure your seatbelts are properly fastened. Thank you."

By now, a total silence had gripped the three hundred and twenty passengers who simply sat and quietly tried to wish the plane down safely. Some silently muttered a prayer whilst others held hands or tried to comfort children, some of whom began to whimper in fear. They could feel the aircraft's gradual descent as their ears responded to the cabin pressure. Those nearest the windows watched apprehensively as the plane broke through the low-lying cloud and lights from the city and the airport became visible. The sight of the lighted city lifted some spirits, but their grip on their partner's hands and reality firmed up considerably as the aircraft came nearer the ground. The plane gradually descended with all on board holding their breath, but just as the wheels touched the runway, it happened!

A massive bolt of lightning hit the front end of the plane which immediately caught fire. Passengers screamed and many tore at their seatbelts in a desperate attempt to get free before the fire reached them. The burning aircraft continued crazily on its way down the runway for a few seconds before a loud explosion occurred causing it to break in two with the first three-quarters of the fuselage veering off the runway before eventually skidding to a halt then vanishing in a mass of flames. The rear portion including the tailplane spun round several times so that the remaining passengers, still strapped in and terrified, saw intermittently the runway, hangars and terminal buildings flash before their eyes. Eventually, after what seemed an age, it skewed off the runway and ground to a halt as the jagged edges of the broken fuselage dug into the soft ground of the surrounding area. It was at this point as the wailing sirens of the rescue vehicles sounded in his ears that Alan Townsend lost consciousness.

Not that he was aware of the time lag, but two days later, he slowly opened his eyes and tried to focus on where he was and what had happened to him. Vaguely, he recalled the plane crash but little else prior to it and certainly nothing thereafter. He was in hospital, that much he managed to understand, partially propped up in bed with tubes and bandages very much in evidence, though as far as he could make out, there were no serious breakages, just a large lump on his forehead that still felt very painful caused, he assumed, by the collision with the seat in front that had knocked him out. As his eyes gradually focused, he became aware of two figures stood at the end of his bed silently watching him. Though his vision was still somewhat blurred due to concussion, he managed to make out that one was a man and the other a woman, both wearing the uniform of the airline he had flown with on his fateful holiday. Seeing that Alan had regained consciousness, the man spoke.

"Good afternoon, Mr Townsend, I hope you're feeling a little better. Brenda and I are visiting the surviving passengers to see if there's anything they need or we might do for them."

Alan blinked almost absentmindedly then nodded his understanding.

"What happened? Did many survive then?"

His partially mumbled question was more in hope than expectation as he began to recall the terrifying moments immediately prior to his own passing out. At first, the man remained silent, but then replied sombrely.

"I'm afraid it was very bad. Only forty-eight of you, all in the rear seats, survived. Some two hundred and eighty souls perished along with most of the crew."

It was at the mention of 'the crew' that Alan became alert.

"But what about Eleanor? Did Eleanor escape?"

At this, the two uniformed visitors looked quizzically at him.

"Who's Eleanor? Is she a relative or friend who was with you?"

This obtuseness made Alan a little irritable and he responded sharply.

"No, No! She was one of the cabin crew. She suggested I change seats. She saved my life. For God's sake tell me she survived!"

At this, the two visitors remained silent for some time until the women hesitantly responded.

"I'm sorry, Mr Townsend, but there was no Eleanor among the cabin crew, I can assure you."

"Yes, there was!" he snapped back "Her name was Eleanor Swift; she told me quite clearly. Please tell me she's all right"

At this juncture, a nurse, sensing her patient was becoming overexcited, came across and politely asked the two visitors to leave then set about calming down the agitated young man with the help of a mild sedative which eventually caused him to drowsily fall asleep.

Alan Townsend switched off his computer, stood up and reached for his jacket off a nearby coat rack. It was lunchtime which meant he was about to walk over the road and find that pleasant little café he had discovered on the first day he'd started his new job almost a month ago having recovered completely from his air crash experience. Pushing open the glass doors of the insurance office, he stepped out into the bright cool autumn sunlight, crossed the road into Piccadilly before turning into a side street down which he found his special eating establishment. Once perched on a stool at the counter, he soon had placed before him his regular simple repast of two eggs on toast accompanied by a mug of steaming hot coffee into which he stirred three large spoonfuls of sugar. Taking out a newspaper from the pocket of his jacket, he laid it half-folded on the counter before commencing his meal.

Half an hour later and fully sated, he refolded the paper, placed it back into his jacket pocket, then slid off the stool before turning to make for the exit door but instead suddenly froze on the spot. Along the main window of the café stood a row of two-seater small tables at one of which was seated a woman, a woman whom Alan recognised instantly. It was Eleanor Swift! Just for a moment, he hesitated unable to take in the moment of surprise. She was alone just staring out of the window a half-empty coffee cup on the table in front of her. Partially recovered from the shock, he stepped forward and stood close to her table.

"Eleanor, so you did escape after all. It's lovely to see you again."

The woman turned her head and looked at him but there was no smile of recognition in return. She appeared to be somewhat perplexed to the extent a slight frown seemed to form in her expression.

"I'm sorry young man, but should I know you?"

Now it was his turn to look perplexed. How could she not remember the person whose life she'd saved by intentionally causing him to change seats on that fatal flight two months ago? He tried again:

"I'm one of the survivors off that Heathrow crash we were on; surely you remember? You're Eleanor Swift surely; the air hostess who saved my life. I wouldn't be here now if it wasn't for you."

This time his words seemed to register some understanding, but there was still no smile nor look of recognition on the woman's face. Instead, she sat back still watching him steadily before she spoke again.

"Sit down for a moment, young man, and tell me your name."

Alan did as he was requested.

"I'm Alan Townsend, and I was on the flight from Barcelona which crashed at Heathrow a couple of months ago. Surely you remember me."

At this, the woman seemed to relax somewhat and he thought he detected a slight smile register on her face.

"Firstly, Alan Townsend, I'm not Eleanor Swift, although I can quite understand why you mistook me for her. You see, Eleanor was my twin sister so it was quite usual for people who saw us singly to confuse one with the other. However, Eleanor died five years ago in a plane crash similar to the one you recently survived."

At this, Alan could only shake his head in disbelief, so dumbfounded was he at what was said, but did not try to interrupt.

"She was on what would have been her last official duty before being grounded in order to take over the job of training supervisor for the airline's hostesses. It was the far eastern run to Singapore, but the plane crashed in a storm at Bangkok Airport." The woman hesitated for a moment as though emotion was about to overcome her, but she recovered and continued her story, "Eleanor did, in fact, initially survive and dragged out an injured passenger, but Eleanor being Eleanor, that wasn't enough; she went back in to the plane several times to rescue more survivors. Eventually, she went back once too often. The plane burst into flames then exploded." A further brief pause ensued before the woman concluded, "Eleanor received a commendation for her bravery; we have it framed at home. It's all we have left of her, you see."

Alan remained in stunned silence simply unable to think of anything to say, his hands, which lay on the table before him, tightened in fraught despair. It was the woman who again spoke when the silence was eventually broken.

"So you see, young man, whatever you saw on your flight that day, it certainly wasn't my sister Eleanor, although what you describe happened was just the sort of thing she'd seek to do if it was going to help someone."

"But I'm sure…"

His intended response was interrupted by the woman placing her hand on his before pressing firmly but gently in a manner that instantly reminded him of a similar moment some two months ago. She looked at him directly but with a soft understanding that told him she was only too aware of his thoughts at that moment.

"Alan, let's leave it there, shall we? You keep your memories of what occurred on your flight that day and thank you for letting me share them with you. Maybe it will enable me to think that somehow Eleanor is still, in her own way, doing what she'd done for most of her life—helping people."

With that, the woman turned her head and once again stared blankly out of the window. Alan knew instantly that the conversation was over. Uttering a stifled word of goodbye, he took his leave making his way out of the door and in the general direction of Piccadilly and ultimately his place of work.

As he turned on his computer in preparation for recommencing work, Alan made himself a promise. Though not remotely religious in any way, he would, that night, say a brief prayer for Eleanor Swift as a thank you for her brief but critical intervention in his short life that enabled him to go on believing in the future.

Queen of Hearts

I remember the journey well. It was one I had made many times during my forty-odd years working in the city of Manchester but one that was so far removed in its experience from all the others that I feel bound to record its events in case, though given the nature of what happened this would be most unlikely, the experience faded from my memory.

Having left the office as usual just before 5:45 pm, it was my habit to walk across the city and make my way to Piccadilly railway station in order to catch the 6:30 pm train which would take me to my home in Knutsford, a small market town in East Cheshire. Normally this routine would give me plenty of time to achieve my objective, but on this occasion, various hold-ups at crossings and junctions along with several traffic jams conspired to delay my progress. This resulted in an increased anxiety on my part that I might miss my train which in turn caused me to quicken my pace in an effort to compensate for my delay. The result of this was that, though I arrived on the platform in time, I was somewhat out of breath. Climbing into the carriage and pulling the door closed, I made for my usual seat at the far window which enabled me to watch the activity on the opposite platform, something I liked to do whilst waiting for the train to depart.

Having settled in my seat and placed my briefcase beside me, I tried as best I could to catch my breath and return to a normal breathing pattern. Unfortunately, being but one year from retirement in my mid-sixties, this proved somewhat more difficult than it once would have done.

"You seem a little distressed; are you all right?"

Glancing up, I saw opposite me a mature lady of what I took to be similar years to myself. She had neatly groomed silvery grey hair, blue eyes and wore a small hat somewhat jauntily askew for such an elegant person. She was smiling at me clearly slightly amused at my perceived 'distress'.

"Yes, I'm alright, really; just a little out of breath due to my exertions in order not to miss the train. Unfortunately, there was quite a lot of congestion crossing the city."

She nodded her understanding, but the smile still lingered across what I felt must have been a pretty face in her younger days. The train started its journey, and I once again attempted to settle down and watch the activity on the opposite platform as we left the station. However, my solitary travelling companion was in no mood to grant me such an indulgence.

"Are you going far?"

The abruptness of the question clearly demanded a reply. Politely I responded.

"Not really; I'll be getting off at Knutsford. That's a small market town…"

"I know where Knutsford is; but you are from Manchester, aren't you?"

I was getting the impression that my companion was attempting to lead or direct the conversation, but strangely enough, I appeared equally willing to respond positively and at some length. This, I should emphasise, was quite out of character for me, a usually taciturn person.

"Originally, yes. I was born in Longsight on the corner of Hamilton Road and Mentor Street. It was a fairly large house, and my mother used it to take in lodgers during the depression: students, travellers and the like."

"But you didn't stay there, did you?"

Though a question, this sounded more like a statement of fact, but in this case, she was correct.

"No, you're right. It seemed mother had a propensity to move on when she was young, and this time, we moved to Hollinwood, Oldham Road, to be precise, where mother took over the management of a public house of all things: a hostelry called 'Help the Poor Struggler'."

"I assume this was also a stay of limited duration."

The woman seemed anxious to move her enquiries along quickly. I was beginning to think she had some sort of ulterior motive in her questioning, but nonetheless, I continued.

"Indeed. It was 1939, and war was declared during our stay there, but as you imply, the stay was not very long. I was only about six or seven years old at the time, but I remember—probably some two years or so later when my mother sought fit to undertake another move—enjoying a journey sitting next to the driver of a horse and cart in which most of our furniture and belongings rested. You'll be aware that at that time, petrol was rationed and very scarce so one found whatever alternative means of transport available."

A further nod from my travelling companion indicated she was paying close attention.

"And where did this quaint form of transport deposit you this time?"

At this moment in time, our train was just pulling into Stockport Station. We were momentarily distracted by the opening and slamming of doors before the stationmaster's whistle sent us on our way once more. I recommenced the tale.

"Well, to cut a long story short, after yet another move, we ended up in West Didsbury, South Manchester: firstly in Lansdowne Road then, ultimately, Central Road. Oddly enough, we remained there for quite a number of years until I married and left home. In fact, my mother ended her days there."

There was a brief silence for a while as though the woman was absorbing or trying to make sense of what she'd been told. The silence didn't last very long, though, and the questioning became even more direct.

"I think I faintly remember something about Central Road. What is your name, by the way?"

"Deric; and you?"

There was what seemed a reluctance and hesitation before she answered.

"Rose. Did you attend school in the area?"

"My brother, who was some four years older than me, and I both attended an elementary school in Withington about half a mile away. It was called Old Moat Lane—quite new at the time, as a matter of fact, built about 1935 although it had recently suffered bomb damage."

At this, the woman seemed to become even more interested and leaned forward slightly in her seat. It was then that I felt I might have met her before. Not recently but some time ago. There was something about her features that I faintly recognised, but at that moment, I couldn't place her. The questioning intensified.

"Can you remember the names of any of your teachers at Old Moat Lane?"

I shook my head in mock despair at such 'long ago' interrogation.

"Well, as far as I recall a Mr Roberts was head, Mr Rogers was our form master in the later years, Mr McDonald took us for PT and science as well as games."

"What about the women teachers; do you recall any of them?"

This seemed a strange question, and I did not grasp its intent until much later. Thinking hard, I finally responded.

"I seem to recall a Miss Allen who took the girls for PT and sports and a Miss Seymour who seemed to be an all-round general tutor, but I don't recall any... Oh wait a minute, there was a rather crusty old thing called Miss Belben; she took us for music and drama as well."

This seemed to capture my companion's interest even more.

"Drama, that's interesting. Were you a budding thespian then?"

I laughed and shook my head.

"Hardly; my only claim to fame on the boards was to play the Mad Hatter in Miss Belben's production of *Alice in Wonderland* sporting a large hat ticketed 'This size 10/6'"

"Shouldn't that be fifty-two and a half pence now?" she quipped.

We both laughed at the thought, but she didn't lose the thread of her questioning. As the train slowed to a stop at Cheadle Station, the inquisition continued.

"And what about your school friends; do you remember or have you seen any of them since?"

I paused momentarily and watched her eager face as she questioned me. I was now even more convinced that I'd seen her somewhere, sometime long ago and equally convinced she already knew more about me than she was letting on. Nevertheless, I answered her latest enquiry.

"As it happens, I attended a school reunion last year and met quite a few old friends."

"Oh? That must have been quite an experience."

I remained silently thoughtful once more as the train pulled away recommencing its journey. There were still a couple of stops before my intended disembarkation at Knutsford.

"Yes, it was, but also a little sad when I was told that one or two of my former acquaintances had died. Reminds you of your own mortality somewhat."

I noticed as I said this, the woman bit her lip and seemed to repress some sort of inner emotion. But it was only a moment's relapse, however, before she brightened up and continued the 'inquisition'.

"This play, *Alice in Wonderland*, wasn't it; can you remember who played the other parts besides your Mad Hatter's star billing?"

The phrase was intentionally humorous, intended to hide the previous show of inner sadness. Her question, however, had taxed my failing memory to the limit. Half a century's intervention hadn't made it any easier to try and remember the names of a bunch of former fifteen-year-old schoolboys and girls.

"You've certainly put my powers of recollection to the test this time. Wait now, let me see. John Morley, he was the school captain, played the Gryphon. That's right, and a chap called Brian Hopley was the Dormouse and then Edwin Williams…"

"But can you remember who played The Queen?"

Her abrupt interruption convinced me at that point my original suspicions that she was leading up to something were not unfounded. As I looked at her then I became even more positive I had seen her somewhere before but just then it eluded me. I strained my memory to answer her question before eventually I recalled the name.

"It was Rose, Rose Pennington. I remember now. She lived in our road. I always thought she had a soft spot for me. That's what some classmates told me anyway. Come to think of it, I had one for her too. So long ago now, I'd quite forgotten."

"And did you ever tell her—about your feelings, I mean?"

The words were almost whispered as she looked straight at me in a manner that bordered on entreaty.

"No, I didn't; I never got round to it, you see. We were so young, and there was always so many things to distract you when you're young, aren't there?"

The woman smiled. It was a sad smile as though she recalled some sort of loss long ago and had just remembered it once more.

"You really should have told her; I'm sure she would have understood."

It was at that moment I remembered—remembered who she was and where I knew her from. It was Rose; she had said her name was Rose, hadn't she? But not mentioned her second…

"This is my stop; I'm getting off here."

She spoke the words as she left her seat and, just for a moment, stood looking at me.

"Goodbye, it's been so nice talking to you."

Turning she made her way to the door as I sat looking after her stunned by what had occurred. But there was one more poignant moment of this encounter to record as she stopped and turned towards me again.

"Will you do something for me, Deric?"

Still bemused by it all I nodded.

"Yes, of course, if I'm able. What is it?"

"Leave the train before it reaches Knutsford. Please promise me you'll do that, won't you?"

Without waiting for a reply, she turned, opened the carriage door and stepped down on to the platform before disappearing into the throng of people heading for the exit. At that moment, I was totally confused and scared. Confused by what she had said when leaving the train and scared because I recalled being told at the school reunion last year that Rose Pennington had died of cancer several years previously.

The train started to pull away, and I noticed that we were leaving Altrincham which left only one more station before Knutsford and that was Wilmslow. I sat looking out of the window as the train gathered speed. I knew it would be less than ten minutes before we reached Wilmslow, the place where I would have to make a decision. I tried to recall her parting words; what was it she had said? "Leave the train before it reaches Knutsford. Please promise me you'll do that, won't you?" Why on earth did she say that? Was I imagining it all? For the first time in my life, my hard-boiled scepticism of all things supernatural was being challenged. I'd never before countenanced such a thing and always scoffed at people who said they had 'seen things'. As the train raced through a tunnel, I looked at my reflection in the window; except it wasn't my face looking back at me it was hers.

The train sped onwards eating up the miles until I sensed it begin to slow down as the driver applied his brakes. I could just see ahead, as I peered into the darkness, the lights of the station begin to appear. What was I to do? Leave the train several miles before my own normal stop as I had promised Rose or dismiss the whole thing as a silly temporary delusion and do the sensible thing and remain on until Knutsford? As the train pulled into the station, I saw the large sign for Wilmslow clearly emboldened under the bright platform lamp like some apocalyptic warning. There was no excuse; I had been warned, and I had only a few precious seconds left to make up my mind as the last of the train's doors slammed shut and the departing passengers headed for the exit. I was cold with fear; I felt rooted to the seat unable to move when suddenly I looked through the window, across the line and over to the platform beyond. There she was, standing under a flickering fluorescent lamp looking straight at me, her face still bearing that sad, pleading look of entreaty. It was enough! As the whistle blew, I snatched up my briefcase and made for the door. Even as I pressed the lock pushing the door open, the train started to move. Just in time, I jumped onto the platform almost falling as I did so.

"Steady on there, Sir" the porter shouted as he slammed the door closed. "Could've 'done yerself an injury doin' that."

As the train pulled away, I stood there watching until the last carriage had passed; then I stared across at the opposite platform and the flickering fluorescent light. She had gone. Somehow, I knew at that moment, I would never see her again. For whatever purpose she had delivered her message and it was for me to work out what it was all about. Once on the platform, reality began to dawn, and I cursed myself for being so gullible. Now what? Here I was the lone occupier of the southbound platform on Wilmslow Station, several miles from my intended destination, all because I'd succumbed to what was more than likely a hallucinatory experience of meeting someone, I hadn't seen for more than half a century. Still cursing, I turned up the collar on my overcoat against the cold autumn chill and headed towards the exit. I made my way down the station approach and then in the general direction of the town. It was almost 7:30 pm, and by the time I'd waited for the next bus to Knutsford and suffered the boredom of the circuitous route, I knew it would take it would probably be near enough to nine o'clock which meant I'd be very late. I didn't have a mobile phone then so there was no way of letting my wife know I'd be late. *Damn! What a fool I'd been.* Arriving at the bus station, the timetable confirmed there would be a half hour's wait before the next bus. Annoyed and thoroughly browned off, I sat down on a nearby bench and waited.

Stepping off the bus at Knutsford, I checked my watch which indicated a few minutes after nine much as I'd anticipated. Since the stop was at the bottom of my road, I stepped out smartly in an attempt to compensate for the lateness already incurred and arrive home as soon as possible. Eventually, I turned into the driveway whilst fumbling in my pocket for the door key. I needn't have bothered. As I approached, the door opened suddenly to reveal my wife standing there sobbing uncontrollably, her face crimson and blotched with constant crying.

"Oh, my God, I thought you were dead. My God, my God! Where have…"

In a moment I was with her, holding her shoulders and enquiring as to her distress.

"My dear, what's the matter? What's happened? You're in a dreadful state."

So upset was she, my wife was unable to speak further but merely took my hand before leading me inside, down the hall and into our sitting room where she stood, still sobbing, and pointing to the television with her other hand. Instantly, I could see there had been some sort of disaster. Railway carriages were shown crumpled and slewed across the tracks surrounded by tangled wreckage whilst firemen desperately tugged at the doors or smashed the windows with their axes in order to release the passengers trapped inside. The monotone voice of the newsreader gave intermittent details of what had occurred.

"Bad railway accident outside Knutsford… Six thirty from Piccadilly, Manchester, left the line… Crossed the tracks before hitting a stone bridge… Fatalities expected with many more injured."

"I thought you'd been badly injured or even…"

I squeezed my wife's hand reassuringly.

"No my dear; I left the train at Wilmslow and came home by bus."

She glanced up at me enquiringly.

"But why? You always…"

"Had to drop something off at the bank's night safe," I lied.

We stood watching the macabre scene for a little longer unable to take our eyes off the dreadful events that I avoided only by the intervention of a long-dead former school friend whom I had last seen alive more than half a century ago. Gradually, my wife calmed down reassured by the fact I was now safely home even if considerably late.

"I'll go and put your dinner on the table in the kitchen and give you a call when it's ready."

So saying, she made her way out into the hall as I sat down on the settee still somewhat transfixed by the television but also mindful of recent events during my journey home. It was then I noticed that my wife had been playing patience as she sometimes did when awaiting my return home. On the long glass table nearby were four rows of cards set out in neat lines, all facing upwards. All, that is, except one solitary card yet not played and lying face down below the others. After hesitating momentarily I reached out until my hand hovered just above the card in question before slowly turning it over. There, staring up at me was The Queen of Hearts, the significance of which hit me straightaway. Instantly, I thought of Rose and tried to remember what she'd said as I was listing the members in our school play.

"But can you remember who played the Queen?" she had asked most emphatically. I smiled to myself as I pictured her.

"Oh yes, Rose, I can. And you played it so well."

Relative Disclosure

Throughout my entire life, I had always expressed a strong disbelief bordering on aversion for all things supernatural or relating to the occult and those who professed an ability to speak or communicate with the dead. Such aversion included séances along with the mediums themselves who I felt were either completely delusional or absolute charlatans. This being so, it was all the more bizarre and incomprehensible that one late afternoon in early January, I found myself ascending the front steps of a large detached house in the suburbs of Hampstead for the very purpose of attending one of these sessions, although, I would hasten to add, much against my will. It came about due to a friend of mine, having suffered a close bereavement, wishing to try and reach or communicate with his departed relative and, not wishing to go alone, eventually persuaded me to accompany him despite his being aware of my deep scepticism. So it was with some uncertainty that I followed my friend into the hallway of the establishment where we divested ourselves of our coats before being ushered into a large reception room which afforded little light other than three wall lights that threw out a dim illumination that enabled us to make out a large round table in the centre of the room around which six or seven people were already seated. In addition to the occupants referred to, sat an elderly looking woman I took to be the medium who was watching the proceedings with an imperious gaze indicating she was anxious for all to settle before she commenced proceedings. When my friend and I were eventually seated, the medium spoke:

"Would everyone place both their hands palms-down before them on the table and ensure that each little finger touches their neighbour's equivalent finger on either side of them thus completing a connecting circle. Now, when I commence trying to communicate with those 'on the other side', there must be complete silence and no one should speak unless they are directly addressed no matter what I do or say. Is that firmly understood?"

Having supervised her instructions had been adequately carried out, the medium then sat bolt upright in her chair and threw back her head. For some time, she remained silent as her upwardly tilted face seemed to stare at the ceiling above her. After a while, she started to tremble and was heard to mumble incomprehensibly whilst the rest of us dutifully observed her instructions to say nothing. At last, she seemed to recover control over her movements and sat staring across the room at the far wall before asking whether anyone in the room knew a certain name. There was a positive response after which the medium assured the person in the room her deceased relative wished to assure her all was well with the departed and no one should worry. A similar circumstance occurred some ten or fifteen minutes later when the target of the medium's communication was informed, she need not worry about her recently departed mother who had 'arrived safely on the other side'. The séance continued in this vein for more than an hour with some messages acknowledged whilst others were not.

All this time as a complete disbeliever, it was all I could do not to intervene and dismiss the entire proceedings as false, but having promised my friend I would stay neutral, I instead remained silent whilst mentally cursing myself for ever having agreed to attend such proceedings. It was about this time, however, when I received what could only be described as a totally unexpected shock.

As I sat there wishing the time would go more quickly so I could get home to the comforts of a warm fireside the medium spoke again.

"Does anyone in this room recognise the name _____?"

The name hit me like a fierce blow to the head. It was that of my family on my Father's side, a Lithuanian name my mother never used though she lived with him for more than twenty years before his death. She instead chose a totally different English-sounding name and that is what appears on both mine and my brother's birth certificates and indeed the one I have used all my life and am still currently known by. There was no way this woman nor anybody else could have possibly known or heard that Lithuanian name in connection with myself. I remained silent for a while, stunned by the unexpected nature of the question.

As if frustrated by the initial lack of response, the medium sharply repeated the question as her face stared up at the ceiling. After a brief delay, I answered in the affirmative before she spoke again.

"Your great-grandfather has something he wishes to impart to you. He says it's something he has never disclosed before and has suffered torment for more than a century unable to clear his conscious."

She fell silent for a while as I felt the first pangs of apprehension creep over me caused by the very supernatural genre, I had steadfastly refused to recognise all my life. The medium then continued.

"You are to visit the house in which he once lived where all will be revealed to you."

That completed all she had to say, and shortly afterwards, she woke from her apparent trance before announcing the séance was at an end. As I searched for my coat on the hall stand, I sensed my friend was less than content. It was he who had expected to receive a communication, not his sceptical, unbelieving friend. It was something of an uncomfortable journey home until we parted company near his house.

I gave no further thought to the events of that afternoon over the next couple of weeks as I was kept busy in both my business and also my domestic circumstances. But one day, sat alone in my study, I started to recall what the medium had said with particular reference to the supposed communication of my late great-grandfather and his wish to impart something to me though I had never met the man who had died long before I was even born. The mention of my father's family surname also worried me since it had never been used in my lifetime making me curious as to how the medium had repeated it from her alleged communication from 'the other side'. I knew little about my father's side of the family other than that which my mother saw fit to impart. It was obvious, even to a young boy, that she didn't much care for them and rarely took the trouble to contact or associate with them. From what she did tell me, it seems the family came over from

Lithuania towards the end of the 1870's settling in the East End of London not too far from Whitechapel. My great-grandfather became a butcher by professional apprenticeship and later had a stall on Spitalfields Market until, so my mother said, he disappeared towards the end of the 1880's; "Probably went back where he'd come from," was her usual curt explanation. Despite my continued firm scepticism about all matters supernatural, the issue represented a challenge, giving me, so I imagined, the opportunity to disprove the medium's claim as just a hoax.

With the help of the internet, I located the Lithuanian immigrant's society and spoke to its secretary asking whether they could locate a family, past or present, by the name of '_____' and, if possible, where they lived. I did have a distant memory of being taken during the war by my father to see his parents although I had no idea where we went. Nevertheless, it was just possible that the family had remained living in the same place over the intervening years. It was several days later when I received a phone call from the secretary informing me that a family bearing such a name lived not far from Commercial Road East in Walden Street where, it seems, they had resided as long as anyone could remember. A strange feeling of excitement coupled with some apprehension took hold of me on learning this but nevertheless strengthened my determination to follow it through and so prove my point.

Several days after this communication, I set off from Hampstead by car making my way towards the east side of the city eventually pulling up and parking close by Commercial Street East and set off on foot to find Walden Street itself. After some considerable time and several stops for questioning, I found myself walking down the said street searching for the requisite number. Although the majority of the surrounding area had long since been flattened and redeveloped, Walden Street, along with one or two others, seemed to have survived in its original state so that I appeared to have stepped back in time as I trod the rough, broken paving stones that formed the pavement running parallel to the roughly cobbled street itself. Even the old-fashioned lamp posts seemed to hail from a bygone age as did the dowdy terraced houses themselves, many of which were boarded up while others stood vacant with windows broken and, occasionally, a door hanging on its hinges.

Eventually, I found the one I was looking for and after a brief pause knocked on the wooden door and waited for a response. The door opened slowly leaving me facing a man who appeared to be of a similar age to myself which caused me to wonder whether he might, in fact, be a distant cousin of mine given I didn't know which part of my late father's dynasty actually owned the place. I took the initiative in communication.

"I'm one of Anthony Louis's sons. Are you part of the family? I was told I might…"

The man cut me short as he nodded a curt welcome, standing back from the door to allow me to enter. Inside, the journey into the past was emphasised further as I entered a smallish, dowdy room that had been entered straight off the street and seemed to contain little in the way of furniture other than an old dark oak table with four chairs as well as a similarly ageing sideboard against the far wall. There were a few dull sepia photographs of family members on the walls and one or two smaller ones standing on the mantlepiece over the fireplace. All in all, however, the room was, to put it kindly, sparsely furnished, and in present day terms could only be referred to as dour. The man sat down on one of the wooden chairs and bade me do the same after which we remained silently facing one another until he decided to open the conversation. He told me briefly that he was the son of my late uncle Louis, my father's brother, so he was, in fact, my cousin and had inherited the house when Louis died. But then he told me something that immediately linked itself to the medium's words at the séance and caused a cold shiver to pass through me.

"Your great-grandfather went back to Lithuania in the late 1880's but left instructions that if anyone came forward in future years from his grandson's family, they should be given what he had left."

With that, the man crossed the room and knelt down before opening a cupboard under the stairs withdrawing what appeared to be a metal box which he placed on the table before me on his return.

"There's no key as far as I know. He clearly didn't want anyone else to open it. You'll have to work that out yourself. It's been almost 125 years since he made the demand, so heaven only knows what you'll find in there."

I thanked him, picked up the box which didn't seem heavy, then made my way back up the cobbled street towards where I had left the car.

It was some days later when I eventually got round to examining the box which had, in the intervening period, lain on the table in my garden conservatory. I sat for a while looking at it still a little apprehensive as to what I might find given the nature of my great-grandfather's desire to keep its contents so secret. Eventually, picking up the strong metal chisel and hammer I'd recovered from my tool shed, I set about forcing open the box by completely breaking away the old rusted lock.

Opening the lid, my nostrils were assailed by a heavy musty smell that more than adequately indicated the hundred and twenty years or more since its contents had seen the light of day. At first, it was difficult to see just what had merited the heavy secrecy that had been conferred by my late distant relative on the few paltry items that seemed to represent what he wished me to have. There was an old pocket watch and chain which I removed and placed on the table followed by a locket which contained a faded picture of a middle-aged Victorian lady I took to be my great-grandmother. Next, I took out a couple of military medals that related to long ago campaigns in Eastern climes. There was a leather-bound book with a fastener which I placed to one side and lastly a small sheaf of what appeared to be cuttings from various newspapers of the period which I again placed without reading them on the table beside the book. The only remaining items were a number of letters tightly bound with a faded ribbon which I removed leaving me staring down into bottom of the empty dust-laden box still more than a little confused as to what it was my erstwhile relative had wished to 'impart to me'.

After some consideration, I turned my attention first to the letters opening each one carefully before reading the contents which, in most cases, seemed to be merely harmless normal communications from relatives mainly at festive times such as Christmas and Easter. There was one from the Butchers' Guild congratulating him on successfully obtaining admission to its membership, but none of the letters appeared to have any particular relevance to any issue he might wish to communicate to me. I placed the items back into the box one by one until I was left with only the leather-bound book which I laid on the table before me, fingering the clip that secured it. Once again, I felt a sense of apprehension overtake me as I deliberated about opening the book as though I might be better not knowing what were its contents. The words of the medium returned to me as I hesitated, "…something he has never disclosed before and has caused him torment for more than a century."

Eventually, curiosity overcame my apprehension. Unclipping the fastener, I opened the book and flicked through the pages in order to see what I was dealing with. It seemed to be a journal or diary of some kind with dates scribbled in spidery handwriting down the left-hand side of each page but was not a normal diary with regular entries as the dates were sporadic with sometimes several days missed before the next entry. It was, however, when I started to read the entries that the story of my great-grandfather and what he wished to get off his conscience gradually became all too dreadfully apparent. I can do no better, reader, than recount faithfully the journal's content in order to indicate just what I was faced with that day, long ago now, when I was brought face to face with the realisation of what my great-grandfather had done back in the murky past of the late nineteenth century.

28th August 1888

I again had those feelings yesterday. For some time now, I have been getting them usually during the day when working at the market stall. Strange sensations throughout my mind and body as though I was being driven by some unseen force to do things—things I'm not certain of and would prefer not to do. Bad headaches occur, so bad that I often have to leave the stall and walk round in an effort to clear my thoughts. I wish these feelings would stop as I'm not really myself when they start to take hold. I've taken to walking around Whitechapel at night. Last night, I found myself walking near Wilmot Lodging House on Thrawl Street watching the women come and go in between their business; it was late, and I felt they shouldn't be out doing what they do. Damn these sensations! They're driving me insane.

2nd September 1888

I knew it would end badly. On Thursday, I went out again late that night. I found myself on Bucks Row walking in the shadows just watching—watching in case someone came by. Then she appeared as if from nowhere coming towards me. She was smiling as she came. 'Ello,' she says, 'want some company, do yer?' Then the feelings took hold. I'd taken the knife from the stall, the one I cut the beef with, and as she got to me, I bring it out of my cloak and cut straight across her throat. She drops without a sound bleeding like a stuck pig. Then I perform my cutting routine just as I do on the beef. When I left her, she was really opened up from torso to her neck. I ran as the headaches started, and by the time I got home, everything was blacked out until I woke next day.

4th September 1888

I didn't go to the stall yesterday. I slept all day, and when I woke, I walked the streets for a while trying to remember what happened Thursday night. It was then I passed a newsvendor and saw the headlines. I bought a copy and took it home. 'Jesus what have I done?' It said a woman called Mary Ann Nichols had been found dead on Bucks Row at 3:40 am Friday morning 31 August, all cut up and in a terrible mess. These dreadful feelings are taking hold of me, and I don't know what to do.

I stopped reading abruptly and tried to take in fully what I had just read. My great-grandfather had committed murder all those years ago and recorded it in his diary; the diary he had directed me towards through a séance more than 120 years later. At that moment, I still didn't grasp the full significance of what he had done or, indeed, who he was. Instead, morbidly gripped by what I had learned, I recommenced reading.

9th September 1888

I take up my pen once more with a shaking hand to record my latest urge-driven act that occurred in the early hours of Saturday morning. I'd been out walking late on Friday night as is becoming my habit, this time close to Spitalfields, and found myself on Hanbury Street, a narrow badly lit walkway, cobbled and wet with only one dim flickering gaslight on the corner of one end. The woman was standing just beyond the lamp silhouetted by the gaslight, her face shrouded by the turned-down hood of her cape; but she saw me and approached smiling, just as Mary Nichols had done, and uttered a similar invitation.

'Lookin' for naughty girl, are we? Well, I just might...'

Her brief miserable life ended right there and then. My knife cut cleanly across her throat, and she collapsed trying to croak a protest from a blood-filled mouth that wouldn't any more respond. The cutting was more extensive this time as though I took a greater pride in my dreadful actions so that her insides were almost surgically removed before being placed on her shoulder. I found myself not only committing the deed once more but taking great satisfaction in arranging the scene for those who might have the doubtful privilege of finding my handiwork later on. The tensions mounted as the mental blackout began. I turned and made my way homewards clutching my head as the pressures inside threatened to burst it open. Slamming the door behind me, I collapsed on my couch and lost consciousness until the pale light of day crept in through my window and my hazy thoughts attempted to reconstruct what had happened the previous night. Looking down, I saw the knife on the floor beside me triggering the recollection my mind had hitherto failed to respond to. It had occurred again! What was happening to me? What demons had taken control of my thoughts and actions?

12th September 1888

    This time. I was back at the market stall on Monday quite back to normal—normal as I can be these days anyway. I bought a couple of papers from the newsstand on my way in and that night sat in my room reading what I'd done the previous Saturday. It seems the woman's name was Annie Chapman, and according to the papers, she'd been done over 'like the other victim Mary Nichols.' It said it must be the same killer given the state of her when she was found in the back yard of number 29 Hanbury Street. The police were out in force looking for the culprit, but so far there were no clues.

I found myself feeling all excited about it. I cut out some of the comments in the paper and put them together—a sort of killer's personal file. I should be feeling bad about all this but I don't; I'm getting a thrill out of it now I'm becoming notorious-like. But I've got to be careful or I'll start making mistakes and that'd be dangerous. I'll try and leave it alone for a while and see if it all dies down. No point in stirring things up too much and drawing attention to myself.

Once again, I stopped reading and sat back in my chair as my mind desperately tried to cope with what I was reading. I'm not a criminologist but even I knew that there had been some terrible murders in Whitechapel and its surrounding areas back in the 1880's; the place was a known hotbed of crime, poverty and killing. But even then, at that point, I hadn't made what to many others would be an obvious attachment of these events and a very famous spate of murders; that would come later when I'd read further and the diary actually made reference to it. Perhaps I wish to wash the possibility from my mind though what I have been reading appals me, I cannot leave it be. With trembling hands, I take up the diary once again and commence reading.

2nd October 1888

I really pushed the boat out last Saturday! First, I found myself walking in Burner Street, all dark and dingy like with almost no lightin'. I get to a place called Dutfield's Yard near the end, when I see this woman standin' under a dim gaslight. She's clearly waitin' for business, lookin' one way and then the other, her hood pulled down over her face till she sees me an lets it fall back so I can see her clearly. My hand tightens

96

around the handle of the knife under me cloak as I walk towards her and she comes to meet me. Poor wretch; she don't know what awaits her. This time she doesn't even get ter say anything before I wipe the blade across her pretty little throat and down, she goes gasping—dead before she hits the pavement. I leave her there as she is. For some reason, I don't cut her any more but simply walk away feeling excited. This won't do. I need another one before mornin'. I carry on walking, walking, walking, the devil knows where.

I gets to Mitre Square near the City and stand on the corner watching until I sees what I wants ter see. She's crossin' the square a little way on before stoppin' and lookin' around her. She seems nervous and edgy, not like the usual pros all confident and pushy. It's late now and no one's about so I approach her slowly so's not ter scare her. She puts on a nervous smile as she comes ter meet me. Poor sod, she'll soon be a gonner. The knife does its business across her throat, and this time, I fancy meself again at me butchers stall and starts cuttin'. She's a right mess when I've finished, her bits all over the bloody place. Now the headaches are startin'; got ter get home before I blackout. I just about manage it and collapse on the bed before passing out until morning.

I bought several newspapers this time ter read about myself' and what I'd done ter them women. It's all splashed over the front pages how The Ripper struck twice in one night. That's what they call me now, 'The Ripper', and sometimes it's 'The Ripper of Whitechapel' instead. I'm famous for what I've done, and yet they don't know who I am. The police are searchin' for me but getting nowhere because I leave no traces for them ter foller'. It's getting' tight now though, and I better be careful less I makes a mistake and leave a trail.

Those poor bitches were called Elizabeth Stride and Catherine Eddowes, accordin' ter the papers, and now every woman in London is terrified ter go out at night.

That's it then! There's no doubt now as to what I'm reading. What my great-grandfather 'wished to disclose' and had caused him torment even beyond the grave was the fact he himself was Jack the Ripper, one of the most notorious and undetected killers the world has known. The detail, the names along with the times and places were all too accurate for there to have been any doubt about its authenticity. Dumbfounded, I sat there staring down at the faded scrawled handwriting hardly able to take in its full and terrible meaning. I slowly reached into the box and retrieved the clutch of newspapers clippings and leaved through them. Faded and yellow at the edges, they nevertheless summarised each of the terrible crimes my erstwhile relative had committed—printed testimony to his murderous actions more than 120 years ago that had lain undiscovered in this box until he'd gone to such lengths to disclose them to me. My God! What a cursed secret to bequeath his unfortunate great-grandson. How am I to live with such a historical albatross hanging mentally round my person? Despite feeling such despondent wretchedness, I knew there was yet more to learn. Though my initial desire was to fling the diary away, I was compelled to finish this dreadful tale that would haunt me for the rest of my days. Slowly and reluctantly I turned the page before recommencing my reading.

12th November 1888

Last Friday, I went on the prowl again like a murderous wolf lookin' for its prey. Wanderin' round Spitalfields, I walk down Dorset Street before seeing a woman just ahead of me. I follow her and see she turns into a place called Miller's Court—a small group of houses set back a bit. Then she stops outside number thirteen of all places and goes in without fully closin' the door. Thirteen certainly is her unlucky number, I'd say. I watch through a side window as she undresses herself then lies on the bed. She seems half drunk and not really aware of what she's doin', so I creeps in quietly and stands by the bed just watching her lying there snoring heavily. I pulls out the knife I keep hidden under me cloak just as she partly awakens and tries ter scream on seein' me, but I'm too fast for her by half. A quick slice across her throat and the pillow quickly turns red before I start me professional activities which leaves her well-carved by the time I've finished. I puts her clothes neatly over a chair just ter show I really cares about me work, so ter speak, before I leave, closin' the door quietly of course. Out in the street, I'm just startin' ter walk away when somebody shouts across at me, so I starts running and don't stop till I slams me own door behind me. That were too close for my liking so I've been thinking a bit over the last day or two. Mary Jane Kelly (that's her name accordin' ter the papers) might well be me last act, so ter speak. Maybe it's too dangerous now for me ter continue. Maybe I should leave and go back home ter Vilnius; it's been a long time since I've seen the old place, and I reckon it'll be a whole lot safer there for me. That's what I'll do then; take meself back to Lithuania so's they can't trace me.

14th November 1888

This'll probably be me last entry as I've booked a passage back home for next week. Told the family I'm goin' for a change and a rest, but I won't be returning no more.

It seems people have been tryin' ter copy me by writing ter the police pretending to be me and signing letters and saucy postcards and the like using me nickname Jack or The Ripper, but that's somthin' I'd never do cos' it'd be too dangerous. The press like it though; gives them lots ter write about and speculate over and also it sells lots of papers for them too.

This diary will be a problem though. I want it left for posterity so ter speak. Perhaps it'll be read a hundred years from now by me great-grandchildren after I'm long in the ground. I'll leave it secure but where it can be found with instructions that only a future great-grandchild must open it up and find he's the distant descendent of one of the most infamous murderers of all time. And me? If there's any truth in some sort of life beyond then there's only one place, I'll be goin' that's for sure and it won't be up there, so I'd better sign off and leave me memoirs to whoever gets ter open the box. So goodbye Whitechapel; keep lookin' you coppers but yer' won't find me.

Yours, Jack.

It was a week or so later when, alone in the house, I went outside and down to the bottom of the garden carrying the diary and newspaper cuttings to where my refuse incinerator stood lit and ready. It had taken no serious thought as to what must happen to this incendiary journal that, if disclosed, would bring the entire world's press to my door with God knows what consequences to follow. I myself would, of course, still have to live with the dreadful and evil bequest my deceased great-grandfather had left me, and I had no doubt that its memory would remain burned into my very soul; something I would have to carry with me to the grave. I stood for a moment staring down into the dancing flames before dropping the cuttings into them and watched them quickly devoured. I hesitated a little further fingering the journal as I mentally recalled its dreadful contents and the first time I read them, realising that when it was destroyed what would have been the most dramatic crime story never told would vanish with it. Taking a deep breath, I tossed the journal into the fire and watched as the flames licked round the binding before slowly consuming the pages which first turned brown with the heat before bursting into flames and eventually curling up into a black nothingness.

Once again, I found myself ascending the steps of that same large detached house in Hampstead, drawn there by some inner desire to bring the torment I was experiencing to some sort of conclusion if possible. I went alone on this occasion but followed the ritual of depositing my coat in the hall and entering the dimly lit room with the round table just as I had done previously. The anonymous group of people were already seated as was the same lady medium who watched me impassively as I too took my seat. Hands flat on the table with fingers touching saw the proceedings commence as she slowly went into her trance.

Matters followed a similar pattern as previously before; an hour or so into the evening, she uttered the same sentence she'd spoken in my previous visit.

"Does anyone in this room recognise the name_____?"

I was ready this time with no sudden surprise as before and answered in the affirmative. For a moment or two, she remained silent simply staring upwards as was her wont before she again spoke.

"Your great-grandfather says he feels his torment has now been lifted and his conscience rests clear."

Retrieving my coat later, I walked out into the cool night air turning up my collar as I did so and muttering to myself:

"His torment may be lifted but what about mine?"

Stand and Deliver

It was in the year 1786 late in the month of September that I found myself riding as swiftly as the terrain would allow in order to reach my destination before the already fading light disappeared entirely. I was journeying in South West Devon heading for Launceston where, just outside the town, my distant cousin lived in a small cottage with her two children, a boy and a girl. I was already cursing myself for leaving my departure from my hostelry later than I had intended as the pathways in this part of the county were sparse and desolate and I did not wish to be out in such hostile territory after dark if that could be avoided. As it turned out, my fears were well-founded for as I approached a small woodland through which my narrow pathway ran, a horseman emerged from out of the wood immediately barring my way. His appearance, cloaked, masked and method of address left no doubt as to his calling.

"Stand and deliver. Forfeit your money or your life."

In order to emphasise his demand, he pointed a two-barrelled pistol directly at my heart. In confused desperation, I tried to placate my assailant.

"With respect, Sir, I'm not a wealthy person—merely a legal clerk travelling to visit my cousin in…"

"I care nothing for your station or intentions; hand over your purse now or I'll shoot you first then take it."

It became very clear that any form of remonstration would be useless; this man meant what he said and would carry out his threat with impunity should I attempt to demure. Still holding the rein with one hand, I slowly reached inside my cloak and withdrew my purse which I carefully tossed in his direction. He caught it skilfully and flicked it open before peering inside. All the time, the pistol remained pointing menacingly at my heart. The man grunted:

"You didn't lie about your lack of wealth it seems."

It was at this point as I sat astride my horse trembling and half-expecting the end to be nigh that the man seemed to change his demeanour. Lowering the pistol he eyed me for quite some time through the mask he wore as though uncertain about something.

"You're a man of the law you say"

I nodded. He hesitated for a moment before continuing.

"And would it be that some two years or so ago you testified at the Exeter Assize court in a double murder trial?"

At that moment, a flash of mental recognition crossed my mind,

"Yes, I did, Sir. Which means if I recall aright, you must be…"

In fact, my tale really commences four years earlier in the summer of 1782 when having negotiated three weeks leave from my chambers, I headed by coach from London to Okehampton from where I hired a horse in order to make my way to an inn known as The Raven's Rest several miles to the north of the town having previously negotiated my accommodation by mail. It was my intention to spend some time riding, hunting and fishing during the early weeks before heading south-west to visit a distant cousin I had not seen since schooldays. She had married, bore two children and lived contentedly with them and her husband until a year or so ago when he contracted an infection which worsened despite medication and led to his death leaving his wife to cope as best as she could. On hearing of her plight from a relative, I felt I might call and see whether I could be of some assistance in her plight.

It was late one August night when, after an arduous ride, I knocked sharply on the door of The Raven's Rest Inn. Moments later, I heard the bolts shot back, and the door opened revealing the landlord replete with double candle holder and looking somewhat bleary eyed. Having introduced myself, he nodded, locked the door and bade me follow him up a flight of wooden stairs immediately to the left which led to a wide landing along which he made his way until stopping outside a door which he pushed open and entered. Following him, I watched him silently light two candles, one each side of the bed, then stand back as I placed my travelling bag on the bed.

"Are can get yer some vitals if yer require, Sir, though it's a mite late, yer understand."

I declined his offer having dined earlier saying I was tired from my journey and merely wished to rest. Without further comment, he turned and made his way out closing the door on his exit. The candles had illuminated the room so that I could now assess my new surroundings more clearly. In addition to the four-poster bed, I saw against the wall to the right a wide dressing table on top of which stood a bowl and pitcher of water whilst to the left a large wardrobe covered most of the wall. In addition, there was a leather-bound chair in the centre of the room. The wall opposite my bed was all but covered by a large leaded window that looked out onto the rear courtyard of the inn. Exhausted from my day's journeying, I undressed before climbing into bed where I fell instantly into a sound slumber.

There is little doubt that without disturbance, I would have slept soundly until first light, but unfortunately such an indulgence was not granted me that night. In the early hours, I was rudely awakened by the sound of heavy footfall on the landing outside my door. I didn't count the number, but I would speculate that some ten or twelve heavy steps occurred before they ceased and all was quiet once more. I remained awake for some minutes wondering whether the steps would repeat but no further sound occurred. Eventually, my tiredness prevailed so that I again fell asleep and did not waken until the strong light of an August sun shone through the chinks of the window curtain.

Having completed my toilet, I dressed and went downstairs where the landlord provided me with an adequate repast of ham and cold potatoes accompanied by a tankard of ale. It was later when I found my host alone that I raised the matter of last night's heavy footsteps. At first, he denied all knowledge of such an occurrence, but further close questioning caused him to eventually relent and tell his tale.

"The footsteps yer eared last night, Sir, wos them of the late Jack Tallow, robber, thief an' violent highwayman. He roamed these parts for many years back in the forties an' fifties until he wos caught, tried at the Assizes in Exeter an' anged in late fifty-six. He used this inn as is base, so ter speak, when he wasn't out plyin' is trade so the story goes; bearin' in mind it was all before my time, yer understan'. Anyway, he comes back from time ter time an' wanders round his ole haunts, an' that's what yer eard last night."

As a sceptical person myself when it comes to matters of the occult, I took the landlord's comments with a pinch of salt and thought little more about it.

As intended, I spent the first couple of weeks relaxing by occasionally riding or hunting complemented by a few days quiet fishing before I prepared to undertake the journey south-west in search of my cousin. It was on the day of my intended departure that the event occurred as I sat at one of the tables finishing a light midday repast. Other than the landlord and myself, there were only two other men in the place sat in the far corner talking quietly when through the inn door strode a young man. Tall, broad of shoulder with a head of black, curly hair and dark, piercing eyes, I would say the man was aged close to five and twenty with a countenance that some may have considered handsome. He paused and looked around before choosing a table whose accompanying chair had its back to the wall, faced the staircase with the door immediately to the left, giving the occupant a clear and all-round view of the room. Sitting down, the man ordered some bread and cheese accompanied by a tankard of ale which the landlord served without any conversation passing between them. For the next ten minutes or so, the young stranger ate his meal and paid no heed to any of the room's other occupants.

Moments later, however, the silence was broken by loud conversation between two men descending the staircase. The older of the two was a burly man with a scarred and ruddy face whilst his colleague was much thinner with beady eyes and a sly appearance. Having once reached the bottom of the stairs, the older man stopped, causing his accomplice to do likewise. He then stood momentarily looking directly at the young visitor who was just finishing his meal, and it was clear there was an immediate recognition on his part.

"Well, now, if it isn't our old friend, Jacob. What'r yer doin' in these parts, Jacob? You usually ply yer trade farther south."

The young man took no notice, but having finished his meal, he pushed his plate and tankard to one side, sat back in his chair and observed the speaker more closely. It was when he sat back in his chair that I first noticed the bone-handled pistol tucked into his belt on the right-hand side. He remained silent; this seemed to enrage his tormenter.

"'I'm speakin' ter yer, Jacob. What the hell are yer doin' here; anser' me, damn you, or I'll blow your bleedin' head orf."

Had the man restricted himself merely to taunts and words, no doubt he'd still be alive today. Unfortunately for him, he foolishly attempted to draw his pistol, no doubt to emphasise his threatening language. That was his fatal mistake. Before his hand found the handle of his pistol, the young man drew his own with the speed of a cobra firing one barrel simultaneously. The ball was true and hit the big man flush between the eyes felling him like a pole-axed animal. One would have thought that his colleague, having witnessed the result of his friend's misguided endeavours, would have exercised some restraint—but no. In an effort, no doubt, to seek vengeance, he too reached for his weapon but in vain. The loud report of the second barrel of the young man's pistol sent a ball crashing into the thin man's chest causing him to crumple and fall across the body of his colleague on the floor.

As the pungent smell of cordite filled the room, I glanced at the landlord who was cowering near his bar, his face contorted in abject terror. The two men across the room were also frozen still terrified with fear as we all watched the young man's next move. Replacing the pistol in his belt, he stood up, reached into his waistcoat pocket with two fingers and retrieved a coin which he placed on the table. Nodding to the landlord, the dark-haired gunman turned and made his way outside into the afternoon sunshine. The unhurried nature of his departure coupled with the deadly execution of his shooting told any observer this young man was no amateur but had probably indulged in similar encounters previously.

As soon as the sound of his horse's hooves had faded into the distance, I left my chair and crossed to where the two shot men lay feeling in case there may still be a pulse, but there wasn't. Both men had been clinically dispatched and lay lifeless in a crumpled heap in the centre of the room. Turning to the landlord who was still cowering near his bar, I told him to send for the sheriff as soon as possible to which he stammered a reply indicating the law was at least two hours ride away and he would have to send his stable boy later. Advising him to have the bodies moved to somewhere outside unless he wished his day's trade to vanish, I informed him I was leaving for two or three days but would be back before the weekend. Should the sheriff wish to take a statement, I would certainly be agreeable. Then picking up my travelling bag, I made my way outside round the back to the stable yard where the young livery boy was standing with my horse already saddled as I had requested. Slipping a coin into his hand, I informed him his master required him to undertake a journey later that day, mounted my horse and set off in the general direction of Launceston which I had been informed was some twenty-five miles or so south-west, a distance I calculated at a steady pace would get me there by late afternoon.

It was, in fact, early evening when I rode into the cobbled yard of my cousin's cottage scattering a small group of hens and causing what I assumed was the family's retriever dog to bark what seemed more like a welcome than a warning. Tying my horse to a railing, I was making my way to the front door when it opened suddenly and two flaxen-haired young children about eight or nine years old came running out followed by their mother wiping her hands on her apron. I held her gently for a moment then kissed her lightly on her cheek as she shed a few tears of long-ago recognition. She was still a handsome woman, but I couldn't help but notice the inevitable lines of worry and strain that crossed her otherwise still pretty face, caused no doubt by the loss of her husband so early in life and the heavy responsibilities that had subsequently fallen on her own slight shoulders.

After the initial greetings, she linked my arm and, with the children and dog following behind, entered the cottage. Despite her limited means, my cousin had prepared a nourishing table for my benefit. Cold ham, potatoes and vegetables were followed by home-baked apple pie accompanied by a glass or so of elderberry wine—a fine repast most welcome and appreciated after my long and arduous ride. Later, we all went for a stroll in the nearby woods where my cousin and I walked side by side and talked of our early days together at school, as the children played and searched in the hedgerows occasionally picking flowers which grew wild nearby.

Back at the cottage, we sat in the small garden on a carved wooden bench under an old beech tree as the children played with the dog, throwing a soft knitted toy that the animal retrieved and returned to them on request. It was then that the conversation turned to more serious matters of how my cousin was managing her affairs and what I myself could do to alleviate her difficulties despite my own limited financial position. When the conversation lightened once more, I happened to mention what occurred during my first night at the Raven's Rest some weeks ago; the footsteps as well as the landlord's explanation the following morning. It seems that, in addition to being something of a believer in the supernatural, she had, before her marriage, lived farther north only a mile or two from The Raven's Rest and was, therefore, quite familiar with what occurred at that time. As a consequence, I will let her tell what she had to say in her own words.

"What your landlord said to you, cousin, was broadly true. Jack Tallow plagued the northern aspect of Devon during the thirties and forties, robbing, stealing and holding up coaches when he would rob the travellers of all they had. When he wasn't doing that, he spent a lot of time at The Raven's Rest drinking, gambling and fighting mostly. He was a violent man and even more violent when drunk which was most nights I'd say. Eventually though, he took a step too far. The sheriff and his men set a trap for him one night by riding the coach themselves fully armed so as to jump him when he held it up. He was tried at Exeter Assizes, found guilty of armed robbery and hanged late in September 1756."

"And that was the end of that, I take it?" I concluded.

My cousin hesitated, smiled and slowly shook her head.

"Not quite as simple as that, I'm afraid. You see, something happened shortly before Jack Tallow was caught and hanged."

"What was that then, cousin?"

"One night that August, a lady walked into the inn. Her name was Lady Charlotte Tremain, daughter of Sir Charles Tremain of Tatton Hall Estate in Somerset, a very wealthy landowner. She'd been visiting relatives and friends in south Devon and was making her way back home to Somerset, but unfortunately, she chose to break her journey at that accursed inn, something the poor woman must regret to this very day."

"Why? What on earth happened, cousin?"

"That night, Jack Tallow was in the place heavily drunk as usual. He saw her enter and make her way upstairs to her room. Later that night when all had retired, he went upstairs, kicked down her bedroom door and ravished the poor woman before fleeing on his horse. He was not seen again until his final arrest."

"Oh, my God! What happened after that?"

Back with her family, she gradually recovered, but as a result of the assault, she became pregnant and the following May in 1757 gave birth to a son. Lady Charlotte was a kind Christian soul, and despite what had happened, she insisted on having the child christened which angered her father and the entire family. She was also a very determined woman and, though the local prelate would not hear of such a thing, her father's wealth and influence persuaded a vicar in a distant parish to carry out the ceremony. What's more, she insisted that Jack Tallow's name appeared on the register in order that her son would have a legal father. If it had been left to her, Lady Charlotte would have kept the child, but this was too much for her father and it was spirited away to some orphanage near Bristol."

"And what happened to the lad, cousin; does anybody know?"

"It seems from what I heard, he led a turbulent childhood, moved from one orphanage to another mainly because of his disruptive behaviour. But given what happened to him, what does anyone expect? Anyway, the last I heard was, at the age of sixteen or thereabouts, he was sent to prison for stealing a loaf of bread, but thereafter, nobody seems to know where he went. Probably left the county to start a new life elsewhere, I expect. Who can blame him for that anyway?"

All the time my cousin was speaking, my mind was replaying the events in the Raven's Rest yesterday and a vision of the dark-haired young man who dispatched the two villains that accosted him hung in the background. As a consequence my next question was tinged with no small amount of trepidation as I half-anticipated the answer I'd get.

"Can you recall, cousin, the name Lady Charlotte used to christen her son?"

"Oh, yes, quite clearly. The family tried to keep matters quiet but news travels fast in these parts. She didn't wish to use his father's first name for obvious reasons, but being the Christian soul she was, she called her son Jacob."

The name struck me like a musket ball; "Jacob Tallow," I muttered to myself but not quite enough it seemed.

"What was that, cousin?" she enquired.

I quickly excused myself and dismissed my comments as mere meandering. Fortunately, she didn't press the point.

I spent two pleasant days with my cousin and her children before I left and made my way back to the Raven's Rest where

I discovered the sheriff had eventually shown up and taken statements from the landlord and the two gentlemen in the corner, but nobody had mentioned my presence which meant I was free to make my journey back to London by coach after returning my horse to its owner in Okehampton. I was ready to return to my post as legal clerk in the Inns of Court much refreshed by my period of 'relative' relaxation.

It was almost two years later, as I was examining a legal register of trials pending, when my gaze fell upon one due to be heard at the Exeter Assize Court in three weeks' time— one that immediately brought vividly to mind events that had occurred on my first visit to the county of Devon. The Crown v. Jacob Tallow, concerning the charge of a double murder that occurred in this county in the month of August 1782 at the establishment known as The Raven's Rest.

The moment I read this, I quickly made my way to the office of my chief clerk and told him all I knew about the event. An honest and fair-minded man, he immediately agreed that I must attend the trial and make myself known to counsel for the defence as my evidence could be crucial. On the morning of the appointed day, I met the defence council and gave him my story adding I was willing to enter the witness box if he so desired. After he had made my presence known to the clerk of the court, we sat discussing the matter until he had all the relevant details, he felt necessary. Then he informed me he would hold back my evidence until the very last moment due to the fact the sitting judge was well-known for his prejudice against defence witnesses of known criminals and would seek to discredit my testimony if he learned of it too early. As a consequence, I sat in the well of the court and was able to witness the progress of the trial.

The judge, a red-faced man of uneven temper, had obviously made up his mind from the outset that Jacob Tallow was guilty and should hang. To this effect, he constantly interrupted proceedings and made biased comments intended to sway the jury's mind to his own opinion often undermining witnesses' testimony in the process. In fact, the defence counsel, a wise and wily barrister, had judged him well but played along as patiently as he thought prudent until all the other witnesses had been heard and just before the judge was about to start his summing up. He then called me to the stand and identified me to the court much to the judge's annoyance who then addressed me.

"You are familiar with the law in your own capacity, it would seem?"

"Yes, my Lord, I am."

He grunted his displeasure before waving on the proceedings. Defence counsel then led me into the most telling and revealing way of making things clear to the jury.

"You were present that August day in 1782 when the two victims were shot, I take it?"

"I was, Sir."

"And you saw clearly the whole event and what led up to the shootings?"

"I did indeed, Sir."

"Very well. Will you now, in your own words, tell the court exactly what you saw occur that day."

Quietly but firmly, I outlined the whole event from the accused's arrival at the inn, his ordering of a meal and the quiet unobtrusive way he behaved until the two now-deceased men arrived and started to goad him without cause. I then explained with emphasis how the older man had drawn his pistol but had been clearly outdrawn by the accused in his own defence.

"And are you of the opinion that the accused had no other choice than to act as he did?"

"I am, Sir. If the accused had not done what he did, I have no doubt that it would have been he who we would now be referring to as the deceased."

Despite some cross-examination by the prosecution which failed to sway my testimony, the jury was overwhelmingly convinced of the veracity of what I had said and duly brought in a verdict of not guilty due to self-defence. The judge was clearly enraged but had no option but to acquit the accused and tell him he was free to go. It was then that Jacob Tallow eyed me steadfastly from the dock and, without comment or change of expression, curtly nodded his thanks before turning, descending the steps of the dock and leaving the court.

"You must be…" I stammered a repeat of my original comment, "…Jacob Tallow."

The highwayman did not respond immediately but merely returned the pistol to his waist belt, much to my relief, and kept on watching me intently through the eyeholes in his mask. Then suddenly and without warning, he tossed my purse back to me which I just managed to hold in my trembling hands.

"One good turn deserves another, they say. The slate's clean now, lawyer man, but have a care our paths don't meet again in the future; I may not be quite so accommodating next time."

With that, he turned his horse around and rode swiftly back into the woods from which he had originally appeared, leaving me a relieved and trembling soul quietly muttering a vague incantation of thanks to some invisible superior being whom I didn't even believe existed but at that moment became a suitable target for my deeply felt relief.

It was quite dark when I eventually arrived at my cousin's cottage later that day. Despite this, I was received warmly by her and the children and, as on my previous visit, served a plain but sustaining repast which was most acceptable after such a gruelling and eventful day. Later, after the meal, with the children now safely tucked in bed, we sat together at the kitchen table, dimly lit in soft candlelight, each with a glass of cousin's pleasant elderberry wine and talked quietly but earnestly about matters that concerned us. It was then that I decided to tell her the full story of what had happened to me, starting with my original stay at the Raven's Rest but this time explaining fully the violent altercation between the two villains and Jacob Tallow though, of course, I was not at that time appraised of who he was, my attending his trial and giving evidence on his behalf and lastly, but by no means least, the terrifying encounter I had with him on the way here this very day. As was her wont, my cousin listened intently and without interruption merely nodding occasionally to indicate she understood the purport of my story, and only when I had finished did she make any observation thereon.

"You had a very narrow escape at the hands of highwayman Jacob Tallow, cousin, for which you are no doubt eternally grateful, but there may be a somewhat more pleasant aspect to this encounter after all."

I looked enquiringly at her.

"How so, cousin? What possible good could come out of such an event?"

She gave me one of her endearing smiles, indicating what would follow could be taken with the proverbial pinch of salt if I so wished.

"I know you are, yourself, not in any way superstitious, but I'm minded to tell you of a strong belief in these parts that has been handed down the generations and is still well-founded in the minds of local people to this day."

"And that is?" I matched her smile with my own of amusing disbelief.

"They say, cousin, that should a highwayman exercise forebearance or mercy towards you during an encounter, then you may expect some form of good fortune in the future."

I shook my head playfully confirming to her my lifelong and enduring scepticism of such country tales and superstitions.

"For my part, cousin, Jacob Tallow's unexpected belief in mutual fairness is all the good fortune that I need or expect for the present"

With that I kissed her gently on the forehead before departing to my room to sleep before an early rise the following day and a long journey back to London.

More than a year had passed before what was discussed that night even entered my mind once more. I was summoned to the office of the firm's senior partner one morning without explanation, and it was with some trepidation that I knocked on his door before entering in response to his invitation. Once seated before him, my superior glanced down at some papers he had on his desk before him.

"Does the name James Chandler mean anything to you?"

A moment's reflection brought a positive response as my memory located a connection from the distant past.

"I recall, Sir, it was a name my dear departed mother often mentioned when I was quite young. It was her brother, my uncle, although I never really knew him. Mother always said he had emigrated—to Australia, I think."

My superior allowed himself a smile of indulgence before replying.

"Your uncle certainly went to Australia years ago but it was not emigration that caused his departure. James Chandler was, in fact, transported to Van Diemen's Land for some minor offence of theft. However, after serving his sentence, he travelled to Australia and joined in the early stages of gold prospecting at which, it seems, he was very successful and later, using the proceeds, started a sheep farming business which also seemed to prosper under your uncle's guidance. Suffice it to say that, when he died last year, he had become a very wealthy man."

All the time during my superior's explanation, I had listened politely to what was said, but up to that stage, I had taken little serious interest. Now, at the mention of my uncle's accumulated wealth, a tinge of excitement ran through me. Surely, he hadn't...

"As you say, your mother and her brother were very close and had she survived him, he would no doubt have left her a generous legacy. Instead, deeming it the next best thing he could do, he left the legacy to her son: your good self. The sum involved is £10,000, and I have placed the money in a personal account in your name at Lombard's in the city. Take this letter of authority I've drafted, and you'll be granted immediate access with complete license to use it as you see fit."

I was still in a daze as I left the office clutching the letter on my way to the bank unable to mentally grasp the sheer magnitude of the amount involved, a sum that, previously, I had only associated with wealthy businessmen or titled people.

All that was long ago when the first thing I did was to secure the future of my cousin and her children, a gesture for which she could not thank me enough. I myself am now settled down with wife and family in a pleasant, spacious house sufficiently close to the city thus enabling me to continue my legal profession at the Inns of Court having decided I was still too young to retire and become a country gentleman. I often sit in my study reflecting how good fortune put me in such a privileged position and wishing my mother could have lived to enjoy at least some of her brother's success. But when I do, I'm often carried back in time to the night I knocked at a late August hour on the door of The Raven's Rest Inn where my adventure began and also, if I can't shut it out, the memory of the dusky evening on a lonely Devon roadway when I found myself staring down the barrel of Jacob Tallow's pistol and wondering whether my last moments on this blessed earth were about to expire.

The Final Journey

The elderly man stood shivering at the bus stop and reviewed his position. It was late, much later than he had intended after visiting his daughter and her family who lived five or six miles out of town, but she had persuaded him to stay just a little longer because they had not seen each other for some considerable time and the early part of the visit had been given over to the two grandchildren who similarly felt they had a justified lien on his time. The consequence of this was that he found himself standing at a remote bus stop worried he had missed the last one that was due at about ten minutes to midnight which would mean he was faced with a long walk home that would see him arrive, probably very tired and worn out, in the early hours of the morning. Besides he was neither a young nor a healthy man. Approaching his seventy-eighth year, he suffered bronchially as well as having a mild heart condition, so the prospect of an arduous five or six-mile walk back to town on a cold and windy November night filled him with some apprehension. To make matters worse, it had just started to rain causing him to step back into the shelter where he pulled up his coat collar and stamped his feet in an attempt to ease the chill that seemed to strike up from the cold pavement, a gesture that caused him to start coughing making it difficult for him to catch his breath.

Glancing at his wristwatch, he frowned; it was turned five minutes to twelve, so unless the bus was late the prospect of a long, tiring walk seemed imminent. The rain was constant now driven by occasional gusts of wind which made him retreat even further into the shelter in an attempt to avoid getting wet. He cursed his delay at his daughter's flat but refused to mentally chide her or his dear grandchildren. He had wanted to stay as much as they had desired him to so it was he himself to blame for his current predicament and no one else. With a further desperate glance at the watch, he was about to bow to the inevitable and start walking when he thought he saw something in the distance. Straining his tired eyes and suppressing a further bout of coughing, he peered into the distance and felt sure he saw a faint light approaching. *'Could this be the bus after all?'* Was it late as he had hoped?

As he forced his eyes to concentrate on the light, it grew brighter and he felt a surge of relief pass through him as the shape of a single-decker bus became clearer as it neared the shelter. Stepping forward, he held out his right arm in an attempt to ensure the driver didn't miss him and allowed himself a brief smile of satisfaction when the vehicle began to slow down before stopping. There was a hiss as the automatic door drew back enabling the old man to take the first step whilst holding onto the handrail before hauling himself thankfully up into the inside of the bus where he stood for a moment straining to get back his breath. He was about to reach into his pocket and take out some change when the door hissed shut again and the vehicle began to pull away. Glancing briefly at the driver, he noticed the man was staring straight ahead through his windscreen across which the wipers swept to and fro, so the old man just shrugged and made a mental note to pay his fare when he eventually left the bus later.

Steadying himself by holding the seat rails, he made his way unsteadily down the centre of the bus until he found an empty seat to his right and sat down moving close to the window as he did so. As the vehicle gained speed the man peered out of the window and watched as the landscape passed by. Houses with an occasional light still shining, roadside trees, their leafless branches being blown by the wind, cars parked without lights and, just occasionally, a solitary figure, its head bowed against the wind, hurrying back to the sanctuary of its home. All this the old man observed without having, as yet, taken any notice of his fellow occupants of the bus or the direction it was taking.

Eventually, however, he looked up and stared down the aisle towards the driver at the front of the bus. The man was still staring straight ahead without any noticeable sign of movement as the bus moved swiftly on through the night, the rain hitting the windscreen only to be repelled by the constant agitation of the wipers. It was almost as though the bus was moving by itself, its bright headlight beams piercing the blackness outside. He'd done this journey a hundred times over the last few years so he soon lost interest in the passing landscape and sat back in his seat, tired and already thinking of his bedtime 'nightcap' before he eventually retired. It was then the man suddenly became conscious of something he hadn't noticed before: the silence. He glanced back towards the rear of the bus then briefly, forward again, estimating that the vehicle would be almost three-quarters full, possibly forty or so people all told. Despite this, as far as he could tell, there was no conversation. The only sounds were the low, steady hum of the diesel engine and the constant muffled thud of the windscreen wipers travelling forwards and backwards repeatedly.

For a few moments, he sat back watching and listening, sure that he would shortly catch some segments of conversation the way people converse quietly with one another when travelling late at night, but despite straining his hearing, he could detect no words of conversation whatsoever; every passenger on the bus was sitting in total silence. It was then the old man felt the first sense of unease. He'd tried to convince himself that perhaps his fellow travellers were collectively too tired to converse, and in any case, some might be whispering to one another farther down the bus so he was unable to hear properly; but somehow, he couldn't quite accept such a surmise. The interior of the bus was quite dark as the few small lights that were switched on gave out only a dim glow. Despite this, he looked across at his nearest fellow passengers just across the aisle on the opposite side. The man occupied the nearest seat whilst his female companion sat close to the window. Both looked straight ahead and appeared to make no movement during the few seconds of observation by the old man who then strained his eyes in the dimness to try and make out their faces. It was at that point; he became convinced something was not quite right. Observation of the faces was almost impossible by the bus lights alone, but when the vehicle was temporarily lit when passing a street lamp, he saw the man's face quite plainly. It was white, pallid and the skin seemed wrinkled and taut as he stared unswervingly straight ahead, his body still and motionless as though fixed permanently to the seat. A brief glance at the woman revealed the same circumstance which made them appear similar to two dummies propped up in preparation for the journey.

The old man took a deep breath as he felt a sharp pain tighten across his chest. He knew what this meant as his heart problem returned once again. Reaching in his pocket, he took out a small packet from which he retrieved a tablet before placing it under his tongue then leaning back in his seat in an attempt to regulate his breathing. After a few moments, the pain eased somewhat and his breathing became more regular as he sat looking down the bus as it ploughed its way through the darkness, occasionally lit by the light from a street lamp or the occasional neon sign winking from some shopfront. He took in the row of heads in front of him that seemed to remain still with no movement whatsoever as their owners stared straight ahead apparently unconcerned with anything or anyone either inside or outside the vehicle. The sense of unease that had first presented itself became more pronounced as the old man tried mentally to understand what was happening.

Anxious to seek further clarification, he turned his head around slowly until he was facing the seat behind him then gasped in horror. There, staring straight back at or through him was the face of a much younger man but with all the same aspects of the passengers across the aisle he had observed previously. The eyes were set deep in their sockets, the face sallow and the skin dry and wrinkled while the countenance gave no sign of comprehension or life; in fact, the man was dead! Turning away abruptly, the old man felt his heart beat accelerate and the sharp pain the tablet had temporarily reduced return with greater severity. Rubbing his chest in a desperate attempt at alleviating the pain, his confused mind struggled desperately to come to terms with what he was experiencing. If the man behind was really dead, why hadn't somebody noticed or said something? And what should he himself now do? He couldn't just ignore the situation.

After a few moments, he forced himself back onto his feet and, clutching the seat rails for support, made his way slowly back up towards the rear of the bus. As he progressed down the aisle, he looked at the face of each passenger, first to the left then to the right. To his horror, he found all were the same; each countenance was fixed, sallow with taut skin and eyes sunk deep into their sockets, their gaze, as such, straight ahead. The posture was always the same, upright with head bent slightly forward but in every case no sign of movement. The old man began to tremble with fear as he took in the macabre situation that surrounded him and of which he had suddenly become a part. Turning, he made his way anxiously back towards the front of the bus in a desperate attempt to prove to himself that all the passengers were not the same and that somehow there would be live, normal people occupying seats farther down; but he searched frantically and in vain as each face he examined wore the same pallid deathly appearance as it stared straight ahead, totally without expression as its owner sat rigid in its seat.

In a state of abject panic, the old man eventually found himself stood trembling next to the driver who, like his passengers, wore the same facial death mask and, like them, stared straight ahead without seeing into the stormy blackness ahead. His hands appeared to be gripping the steering wheel, though how he could possibly guide or influence the passage of the bus caused the old man's senses to collapse into further confusion. As he stood there peering now and then into the blackness ahead, a blackness that was still occasionally alleviated by street or shop lights, the situation began to dawn on him. He had become part of some macabre funereal tableau surrounded by cadavers being transported God knows where; he gradually surmised that he himself was destined to become part of it.

As he staggered back to his seat before collapsing into the corner, he tried to think back desperately to what had occurred earlier. Gasping for breath as the pain in his chest tightened, he vaguely recalled leaving his daughter's flat having played with his grandchildren then standing at that cold, desolate bus stop hoping the last bus had not gone. 'But…' he thought through his fading senses, '…this is not the last bus; this is…' As the old man slumped in his seat, the sombre vehicle, which had just left the last of the town's lights behind, ploughed relentlessly onwards into the blackness beyond, its lights still blazing as the windscreen wipers tolled unremittingly to and fro.

The House with a Past

It was customary for the young boy to take the wooded path when returning home from school each afternoon as it bypassed the main road that led from the town and took him to the outskirts of the village in which he lived in a much shorter time than it would otherwise take.

As a final year student at the school, he was allowed to leave class at his choosing provided he attended the requisite lessons that would guide him towards examinations at the end of term.

Late summer made his afternoon walk home a pleasant one during which he took in the beauty of the overhanging trees through whose branches the late sunlight occasionally shone, coupled with patches of wildflowers that grew along the hedgerows and, if he was lucky, a brief glimpse of some scampering animal as it scurried nervously out of sight having been disturbed by the boy's approaching footfall. Having made this journey more times than he could recollect, there was little of the pathway's appearance or hinterland he was not familiar with, so he tended to wander aimlessly without taking much notice of the all too familiar surroundings, observing only when something mildly unusual took his eye.

What took his eye on this occasion was the old abandoned house that stood back some distance from the pathway but could occasionally be seen through gaps in the branches of the surrounding trees and bushes. He was well aware of the house's presence having glimpsed it many times over the years, but somehow, he'd never taken much notice of it other than wonder to himself now and then how long such a sad looking place might have stood unoccupied. This afternoon, however, something made him pause as he came within sight of the old building. For a moment he stood and looked, not knowing just why, after so many casual sightings over the years, he should now take an interest in the place. The fact of the matter was that just as he was passing the spot where it could first be sighted fully, something inside him had registered, and as a consequence, he had stopped and looked up, but for the moment, making no move to advance.

'Curiosity,' he thought. That could be the only rational reason for his sudden and belated interest. Having convinced himself of that fact, he took the first cautious steps off the pathway and into the dense foliage that blocked his advance, pushing away the occasional drooping branch as he went. A few moments later, he found himself standing on the edge of a clearing some twenty yards or so from the building itself. Such close proximity made the house seem even more dilapidated while accentuating its doleful, abandoned appearance.

The house seemed somewhat bigger than he had imagined previously. It was double-fronted with large windows on each side of the front door indicating, probably, spacious rooms beyond. Built primarily of brown sandstone, the top half of the house had been layered with timber, much of which was now showing the result of many years neglect. Across the front of the house stretched a wooden veranda with a set of wide steps leading up to the front door. After a brief pause, the boy made his way slowly forward until he found himself standing at the base of the steps where he hesitated once more before cautiously mounting them thus bringing him face to face with the glass-fronted entrance. So engrained was the frontage with the dirt of many years, he was unable to see into the house. Reaching for the handle, he tentatively gave it a turn before pushing open the door itself which responded to his pressure and stepping inside where he found himself staring down a long hallway off which there were several doors leading to adjacent rooms.

The first thing that struck him was the strong obnoxious stench of dankness which seemed to permeate the whole house, confirming that the place had been uninhabited for a considerable number of years. Layers of dirt and dust covered the floor to such an extent that it partly muffled his own footsteps as he commenced moving down the hallway. He glanced through the doorway immediately to his right into a large and spacious room with a rough brick fireplace on the opposite wall. It had high ceilings with ornate cornices running the entire length of the walls which, themselves, were punctuated by old long-defunct wall light fittings. Like the hallway, the floor was covered in a deep layer of dirt but also a good deal of old plaster which had clearly rotted before falling from both wall and ceiling.

Holding a handkerchief to his nose to keep the stench from his nostrils, the boy made his way out once more into the hall and was about to examine the room opposite when he heard something and stopped abruptly. He could not be certain but thought he heard the sound of soft laughter. In fact, he told himself it sounded like the laughter of two young voices coming from upstairs. For the first time, a feeling of tension entered his being. Not fear as he was not given to superstition or ghost hunting but a feeling that this place may have experienced something unusual in its past—something that perhaps had remained hidden for many years but was there just under the surface. Besides, he was a naturally inquisitive lad and, having almost immediately dismissed the sound as mere imagination, continued his investigation.

A brief examination of the remaining lower rooms revealed only further dust and emptiness, so he turned his attention to the next floor. Stepping gingerly on each stair to avoid accident should it be rotten, he eventually stood on a wide landing off which he could make out perhaps four bedrooms and another which he took, without examination, to be a bathroom. The two front bedrooms looked out onto the clearing as well as the pathway he had used to approach the house initially. At the rear, the windows of each room looked down onto what had once been the back garden but now resembled a small jungle with overgrown bushes and tangled foliage intermingled making progress to what appeared to have been an orchard farther back almost impossible.

The boy stood for some time gazing out onto the overgrown wasteland, trying to imagine just how it may have looked in its prime. He could just make out the remains of a dilapidated wooden fence that traversed the perimeter of the 'garden' and separated it from a field beyond. The trees in the old orchard had almost all died or gone back to the wood so that the entire area gave off a gaunt and lifeless appearance. Just about to turn away from the window, he saw what he took to be the overgrown remains of a well, its low brick superstructure badly crumbled and its wooden winch support almost entirely rotted away. He made a mental note that he would, perhaps, examine the rear garden in greater detail after leaving the house and before heading home.

He turned and made his way towards the door only to have his attention directed to something lying on the floor in the far corner of the room. On examination, it appeared to be a small picture frame, face down and surrounded by broken glass. Stooping down, he carefully lifted the frame with both hands before turning it face upwards. It was, he assumed, the picture of a family: father, mother and two young boys. He stared for some time at what he took to be a brief glimpse into the past and of the house's former occupants. The mother was a slight pale-faced woman with mousy hair cut short to just below the ears. She wore a high-necked blouse and had on a rather elegant wide-brimmed hat. The two boys would be, the intruder inferred, about seven or eight years old and were both dressed identically in long-sleeved V-necked pullovers and open-necked white shirts. The mother and her sons were smiling during the taking of the picture but the father certainly was not. He was a man nearing fifty or so with a narrow, lean face. His hair was thinning and brushed well back and parted in the middle. The eyes seemed to stare almost wildly at the camera from behind a pair of horn-rimmed spectacles. The sight of him made the young boy holding the picture shudder slightly, but for a moment or two, he stared as though transfixed. There was, he thought, something evil about the man though he couldn't quite identify at that moment just what it was. Eventually, he placed the photograph and frame upright on the nearby mantelpiece although he hardly knew why. It had certainly lain where he'd found it for decades and no one was likely to bother reclaiming it now.

Turning, he made his way out of the room, along the landing and then, choosing his steps carefully, down the partly rotted staircase until he stood once more in the hallway. Pulling open the door, he was just about to step outside when he heard it again! This time there was no doubt in his mind. The sound of two young voices emitting a ripple of gentle laughter drifted back down the staircase was as clear as it could be. Swallowing hard, he stepped outside pulling the door closed behind him.

On the veranda, he paused for a moment before recalling his intention made upstairs to briefly examine the back garden before going home. Down the steps and turning left, he traversed the east side of the building before finding himself standing knee-deep in undergrowth at the back of the building and staring at the almost impenetrable wall of vegetation that now represented what had once been a back garden. The orchard beyond was unreachable whilst the old garden shed against what was left of the fence had rotted until there was not much more left than a skeleton door and window frame. To his right was the crumbling remains of the well he'd spotted from the upstairs rear window.

Picking up a thick branch, he stepped over and started pushing away much of the weed and grass which had grown over the well's mouth then peered inside. There appeared to be a couple of layers of bricks blocking the upper part of the shaft so the boy reached down and removed one or two enabling him to see beyond. Below the bricks it appeared the well had been cemented over though much of the mortar had long since started to disintegrate so it was possible to see beyond the debris but not as far as the bottom. He wondered why someone would take the trouble to cement over a well which had once been a feature of the garden. Shrugging his shoulders, he threw down the branch and glanced at his watch. It was getting late and, anyway, he was feeling hungry. Making his way back to the front of the house, he crossed the clearing and picked his way back through the surrounding foliage to the pathway that led homeward—although much of the journey would be taken up with thoughts of an old sepia-coloured photograph and a cemented garden well.

Some days later, the young boy was at home sitting on the settee in the front room watching his mother go through her weekly ritual of dusting and polishing the furniture. A widow in her early forties, she still had a trim figure and could probably pass for someone several years younger. Her husband had been killed in an industrial fatality at work some years previously, and after a period of legal wrangling, she received a substantial lump sum along with a modest pension off which her son and herself managed to live comfortably.

After some time watching his mother's activities, the boy broke the silence by posing a question which, to say the least, took her by surprise.

"Do you know anything about that old house in the wood?"

The effect was instant. Part way through polishing the dining table, she stopped with her hand still pressing the duster to the table's surface but her face looking straight ahead out of the nearby window. Initially, she didn't reply but remained still, almost frozen in time, as though she hoped the question hadn't been asked. It was, however, repeated once more.

"Well, do you? You know, that old place standing back from the pathway. It's in a dreadful state; I saw it the other day."

The mother slowly recovered from her torpor, stood up but remained staring out of the window fumbling with the duster.

"I wouldn't go anywhere near that place if I were you. It's very old and probably dangerous inside."

The words seemed evasive and didn't satisfy her son.

"But do you know anything about it? Who lived there and how long ago?"

The mother saw she was trapped. The question wouldn't go away, so she sat down on one of the dining chairs facing her son. It was some time before she spoke again.

"All anyone knows about that place is what's been handed down over the years by people who've heard it from others—passed on as a form of folklore—but there's nobody alive who can claim to have been living when it happened."

"When it happened? When what happened?"

His mother gestured to her son that he should not interrupt, then continued.

It was said that the family, Anderson I think their name was, came to live there just before the First World War. Quiet people they say—father, mother and two sons aged about eight or nine."

At the mention of two young sons, the listener recalled the old sepia photograph he'd seen but said nothing.

"The father went to war in 1914 like many at the time and saw terrible things which some say affected him badly. He survived, however, unlike a lot of others, and came back after armistice to take up his family life once more. Things seemed all right for a year or two, but then sometime in the early twenties, I think, the mother and her two children disappeared and were never seen again."

The boy, who had been listening with an almost desultory lack of interest, suddenly became alert.

"But what happened, Mother? Surely the police got involved."

The mother smiled wanly.

"Yes, they certainly did, but bear in mind this was some ninety years ago; there wasn't any CSI in those days. Anyway, the husband insisted his wife had taken her things as well as the children and left home and though there were some, including the police, that had grave doubts, they couldn't find or prove anything."

"So what eventually happened to the father? Did he carry on living there? His mother shook her head then, turning, gazed out of the window once more as though looking into the past before answering.

"Only for a short while apparently. It seems he booked himself a passage on some ship about six months later and sailed from Liverpool to Australia. Nobody ever saw sight nor sound of him again, they say."

Her son reflected on what he'd been told for some moments before seeking further information.

"But what about the house? Did anyone else ever live there?"

His mother turned to look at him again.

"As far as I know nobody would take on the place, so it's just stood there rotting ever since." Then fixing her son with a steady gaze she concluded, "So as I've said, I wouldn't go near that place if I were you."

Most of the time between the conversation with his mother and his imminent departure to university that autumn was taken up with preparations: seeking accommodation down south and saying farewells to some of his closer former school friends. Indeed, it was having spent the evening with one such acquaintance but lingering longer than intended that next saw the boy make his way down the steps of the old town bridge and onto the wooded pathway that used to be his regular journey home from school. By the time he commenced making his way along the path that was now partially covered in leaves as the surrounding trees shed their foliage, it was already getting dark; but since the weather was mild and dry, he didn't concern himself.

It was when he arrived at the point where he had last glimpsed the old house that something caught his eye. The trees, having shed a good deal of their leaves, were not now the visual barrier they had been earlier that year so he could see the outline of the house quite clearly; but not only could he see its outline, there was a bright light shining from one of the downstairs windows! The sight of any sort of life or activity in such a long-deserted place made him halt instantly as his mind began to consider the various possibilities for such a strange circumstance. Could someone be living in the place? Surely not, considering the dreadful condition of the house when last he saw it! Maybe someone was investigating just as he had done several weeks ago? But this idea he also dismissed promptly, as the light he could see was far too bright for any torch or lantern. No, there was some other explanation, he told himself; but without further investigation, he couldn't think what it could be.

After further hesitation, his natural curiosity took hold and he stepped off the pathway making a slow but deliberate pathway through the undergrowth, his eyes fixed steadfastly to the bright light emanating from the downstairs window. Moments later, he arrived at the clearing some yards from the front of the house just as he had done previously, but whilst the house at first appeared as he had first encountered it, a moment's observation showed the boy things were far from being the same. Though he stood in semi-darkness broken only by the light from the window, he could tell instantly that the building was not old or dilapidated! It appeared quite new—its woodwork clean and painted, its brickwork smooth and even whilst the veranda and steps were also clean and unbroken. It also appeared from what he could see of it that the garden was neat and tended with bushes trimmed and borders tidily kept.

How could this be? he thought. As his eyes got used to the semi-darkness, he noticed other things that had not been evident when last he visited the place. Around the near side of the house was a motor car, an old-style Ford which the boy estimated would come from the 1920's or '30's, whilst leaning against the front wall underneath the window stood two children's bicycles. As he stared in a state of incredulity and confusion, it started to dawn on him that what he was witnessing was some sort of backward vision of the house, not in its present-day condition, but how it must have looked some eighty or ninety years ago when it was quite new and habited. The thought of habitation suddenly made him wonder who, if anyone, might be currently occupying this surreal looking place. Slowly, he made his way across the clearing, onto the front lawn then on towards the lighted window which appeared not to be curtained at present. By now, he was feeling tense and more than a little afraid with his heart beating at many times its normal rate, but something inside kept urging him onwards as though it was intended that he follow this vision from days gone by to its conclusion.

Eventually, he found himself standing close to the window and peering into the front east side room he had examined when last he visited the house. But where previously there had been layers of dust, dirt and fallen plaster, he now saw a deeply carpeted floor, neatly papered walls with brightly polished light fittings. The whole room was tastefully furnished with a three-piece suite, a sideboard and a well-stocked bookcase whilst in the far end of the room under the rear window was a highly polished dining table and four chairs. From the ceiling hung a large, ornate gilded chandelier, itself the main cause of the bright light that had originally attracted his attention back on the wooded pathway.

The young boy stood, as though in a trance, surveying this flashback transformation of what had been an old dilapidated house into its erstwhile state of relative pomp some nine decades or so ago when, suddenly, the spell was broken by the entry into the room of a figure carrying over his shoulder what, at first, looked to him like a rolled carpet covered in a bedsheet. It was when the figure laid his burden onto the lounge floor that the young observer saw to his horror that it was, in fact, a body. There was just enough of the feet and head showing at each end to confirm this macabre conclusion.

No sooner had the body been deposited than the figure turned and disappeared out of the door leaving the boy numb with fear unable to properly grasp the magnitude of what he was witnessing.

But if he was shocked at the sight before him, his sensitivities were shattered when next the figure appeared in the doorway once more, this time with a similar but somewhat smaller burden. It was, the observer inferred, one of the young boys who was instantly laid beside its mother. The operation was repeated for a third time until the three members of the family lay dead side by side on the carpet of their own living room floor with the father standing over them panting for breath after his murderous exertions. Peering through the window, the boy recognised the face instantly from the old sepia picture he had found upstairs. The narrow lean face, the thinning hair brushed back and parted in the middle, those staring eyes through the horn-rimmed glasses that gave him the wild manic appearance the boy had recoiled from when first he had seen it. Now he was watching him as he had once been; the calendar turned back to the early part of the last century when he had committed these terrible murders and was, presumably, planning the final part of his terrible crime; how to dispose of the bodies without detection.

The watching boy's mind was trying to follow if not anticipate the father's likely next move having seen him bring down the victim's bodies probably from an upstairs room. He sensed they would be taken outside as there was, as far as he could tell, nowhere within the house where they could be safely hidden from any serious investigation. Then he remembered the well in the back garden; could that be it?

As the father, having partially recovered his breath, bent down and lifted the woman's corpse and slung it over his shoulder before turning back towards the door, the young boy left the surreal picture and made his way around the back of the house where he stood close to the well just as the back door opened and the man emerged. The boy had not been wrong; unsteadily the father made his way across the lawn and stopped just in front of the well so close to his observer that, had the scene been contemporary, they could have touched. Then, without hesitation, he lifted the body from his shoulder and fed it into the mouth of the well where it made a dull thud as it hit the bottom. The man stood panting for a while but soon returned to the house from which he again emerged moments later carrying the first of his dead sons' corpses before dropping it down the aperture in a similar manner. This ritual was repeated once more after which the father remained standing by the side of the well his body heaving violently with the exertion, his head slightly bowed as he stared into the blackness of the final resting place of his entire family.

Some moments later, he retired to a small garden bench where he rested for several minutes. It was then that the boy saw, close by, a wheelbarrow filled with what appeared to be thick mortar. After resting, the man rose, took up the handles of the barrow and pushed it to the well. He picked up something from nearby which looked like a solid wooden ring or lid which he fitted some way down the well. Stepping back the man gripped the handles of the barrow once more then slowly tipped the contents into the dark hollow of the well.

The watching boy felt a surge of revulsion run through his entire body at what he had just witnessed and knew only too well what would happen next. Later, the man would place several bricks over the dried cement where they would give the impression the well had been blocked for some considerable time and where they would lie until he, himself, would remove them some ninety years later.

As the man retreated from the well with the wheelbarrow, the vision began to blur as it changed back into the present day with the garden overgrown and the surrounding fence and garden shed returned to their state of dilapidation. The well, into which the unfortunate members of the Anderson family had been entombed, took on its crumbled and overgrown appearance once more, and the young boy was left standing alone and partly traumatised by what he had just experienced. It was some considerable time before he had recovered his composure sufficiently to accept what he had witnessed was some supernatural flashback to a time long gone which had, for some reason, seen fit to replay itself for the benefit of future posterity and that he, presumably by sheer chance, had been pointed in the direction of its replaying. Slowly he turned and made his way to the front of the house, over the garden and the clearing, before threading his way through the foliage onto the pathway that would lead him homeward.

After having finished polishing her front room furniture, the mother made her way into the kitchen where she made herself a pot of tea before seating herself at the kitchen table and pouring herself a cup. She reached for a copy of the local newspaper nearby and pulled it towards her before reading the headline that stared out at her.

"Century Old Local Mystery Solved At Last!"

The article went on to say the mysterious disappearance of three people, the mother and two sons of a family named Anderson, more than ninety years ago had now been satisfactorily solved. It seems that some weeks ago, a young student had walked into the local police station and related some story about having discovered the source of these long-ago disappearances. At first, the station sergeant dismissed the claim until a visiting retired former policeman who overheard the boy's statement intervened. It seems his father had, as a constable in the 1920's, worked on the case and told him about what happened and the unsatisfactory nature of the investigation. On the strength of this, a search of the garden well at the old house in the wood was made and it was then that the skeletal remains of a woman and two young boys were discovered. Forensic tests subsequently proved that they were, indeed, the remains of the unfortunate missing family members of the murderous father who had made his escape by ship to Australia some months after committing the deed.

The mother continued to stare at the headlines for some time before pushing away the paper while directing her gaze out of the window and muttering to herself, "I told him not to go near that place, didn't I; but he wouldn't listen."

Titanic Revisited

The young man strode up the steps of the National Maritime Museum in Greenwich. It was his lunch hour, and he often visited the museum as he was something of a maritime student with a built-in fascination for the sea and all that sailed thereon. Furthermore, he worked in the maritime section of the Board of Trade which further fed his obsession with seafaring. Today, however, he had a special reason for visiting the museum, and the thought of seeing it for the first time instantly quickened his pace. Once through the main doors, he sensed the quietness of the place as he made his way through the first of the high-vaulted rooms containing row upon row of glass cases displaying countless treasures of seafaring occurrences long since past. The young man did not however, on this occasion, pay any attention to such displays. His mind was set upon one special item that had only recently been introduced to the museum and, if his directions were correct, would be displayed in the next room.

On arrival, he scanned the walls keenly until his eyes caught the display for which he was looking. Sitting down on a bench opposite, he stared up admiringly at the strikingly beautiful picture of a large liner cutting its way through the water with three of its four funnels leaving a trail of black smoke streaming behind; the fourth funnel, as any maritime buff worth his salt would know, was merely an air shaft. Because, this wasn't just any cruise liner; this was the Titanic, the latest addition to the White Star Line; the most luxurious ship afloat and, thought by many, to be a direct challenge to the Cunard fleet that currently held the Blue Riband for the Atlantic crossing to New York. As he stared admiringly at this majestic depiction of the Titanic, the young man ran through its well-known statistics that any schoolboy of that era could probably recite. A length of 882 ft with a beam of 92 ft and weighing 46,329 tons, it was certified to carry a maximum of 3,300 passengers and crew—though for its maiden voyage due to commence on 10 April, the figure would be nearer 2,200. Her bulkheads though sound were not individually watertight and…

"She's a real beauty though, isn't she?"

The comment that interrupted his silent deliberations came from beside him though the young man could swear no one else occupied the bench when he first sat down. Glancing to his left, he saw a man sitting barely three feet away and staring up at the picture. Probably in his early fifties, the young man thought, he had a ruddy complexion well-tanned by sun and wind, all of which seemed to indicate a seafaring background. After a moment, the young man answered.

"Yes, she is; big yet elegant and certainly luxurious. Unsinkable, they say."

At this the seafarer seemed to balk.

"Oh no, son. Never believe that. She's made of iron and steel, so should she ever be holed below the waterline, she'd sink alright; sink like a stone she would."

At this, the young man felt a little indignant as though such talk about this great liner was a personal affront.

"But what on earth could possibly sink such a massive and sound vessel, I ask you?"

The man remained silent for a while before offering a reply.

"If yer'd read yer sea history, son, you'd know the answer ter that. It could hit a hidden rock or another ship so it could. Then there's bergs an' growlers, aint there."

At this, the young man looked enquiringly at him. "What do you mean by that then?"

"When she leaves Southampton on 10 April, she'll call at Cherbourg in France then cross over to Queenstown on the west coast of Ireland before setting off up to the North Atlantic and New York."

"Well, what's the problem with that?"

"The problem, son, is that at this time o'year, the North Atlantic is full of massive bergs that 'ave broken away from the main pack an' started to drift south. It probably won't ever 'appen but should she 'it one o'them things then...who knows. See for yourself."

The young man followed the seafarer's gaze back to the picture, at which point, he gasped in horror. No more was the elegant liner cutting majestically through the waves. Instead, its bow was partly submerged, its stern half out of the water incongruously displaying one of its massive propellers whilst hundreds of despairing passengers could be seen clinging to the ship's rails or anything else available to give them temporary hope. In the sea around the stricken vessel were maybe twenty lifeboats, some full, others sparsely so, whilst the surface of the sea around was littered with flotsam that had broken away from the ship. From somewhere on board the Titanic, a distress flare shot skywards in one last despairing attempt to contact vessels that might be in the vicinity.

The young man gasped in despair, "Oh, my God, no; don't let this happen."

He turned to address his interlocutor, but he wasn't there anymore. The seafarer had vanished just as mysteriously as he had first appeared. In desperation, the young man looked back at the picture then gasped in relief. The original scene had been restored; the magnificent ship was once again sailing serenely onwards, its sharp bow cutting through the water like a giant knife.

Relieved, he wiped the perspiration that had formed on his brow with his handkerchief before glancing at his wristwatch that told him his lunch hour was almost ended. Slowly, he rose from his seat and made his way towards the exit and out onto the street beyond.

Once back in the office, the young man hung up his coat and sat down at his desk. Across the room, he saw his boss, Francis Carruthers chief surveyor of major shipping and the man who would, eventually, sign the Titanic's certificate of seaworthiness. Carruthers addressed him without turning round.

"Did you have a good lunch then?"

Yes, thank you. I called in the Maritime Museum to see Titanic's new painting."

"Oh, does it do justice to the ship, do you think?"

"Yes, it does. I'd love to see her before she departs next week."

Carruthers swung round in his chair and passed a thick folder to the young man.

"Well, could I suggest you check through this file once again and make sure we've missed nothing. I need to sign the certificate as soon as possible or your wonderful ship won't be going anywhere. Look sharp now, we haven't got much time."

With that the man turned back to his desk as his young assistant opened the file and commenced reading.

He worked steadily and assiduously checking each page of information most of which he'd seen previously during the file's compilation. It was just when he thought everything was in order that he spotted something. Having turned over to the page covering safety, he studied the question of lifeboat availability and this pulled him up sharply. According to the information on the page, Titanic would carry 20 lifeboats in total. There were fourteen standard ones, each capable of carrying a maximum of 65 people, two emergency cutters, each able to carry 40 persons, and finally, four collapsibles, each one having a maximum capacity of 47 people. The young man quickly did his arithmetic and concluded that the total capacity of these lifeboats, assuming each one was fully loaded, came to 1,178 whereas the estimated likely total of passengers and crew on its maiden voyage stood at 2,229, a shortfall of some 1,051. He double checked the figures several times to make sure he hadn't made a mistake then sat looking down at the page for several minutes before commenting.

"Excuse me, Sir, but have you seen the lifeboat ratio to passengers and crew? There seems to be a considerable shortfall."

Carruthers answered initially without turning round.

"Yes, I have. The figures are correct and in accordance with the owner's wishes."

"But Sir, Titanic would have to sail knowing, in the event of a catastrophe, some 1,051 passengers would not be guaranteed safety."

This time his superior turned his chair around slowly and faced him.

"Surprisingly, the situation is, in fact, adequately covered by current maritime law which, so it seems, lags behind maritime engineering and technology. But as I've already mentioned, it is the wishes of the White Star Line who have approved the ratio. It would appear they do not wish the promenading deck passengers' view interrupting."

The young man could hardly believe what had just been said and simply sat staring at his superior for a while before responding. When he did, he made his own feelings brutally clear whilst still endeavouring to remain courteous to his interlocutor.

"But Sir, surely that is the height of irresponsibility by the owners, putting simple enjoyment of deck-walkers before passengers' safety. And what about yourself? You'd be knowingly signing a certificate of seaworthiness whilst being aware that over a thousand passengers could be in mortal danger."

Carruthers tried to evade the issue by questioning the likelihood of a catastrophe occurring to such a massive seagoing leviathan.

"Let's be fair; what on earth could possibly happen to such a wonderful piece of maritime engineering? The Titanic is well-nigh unsinkable, for God's sake…"

At this, the young man suddenly recalled the words of the tanned and ruddy-faced seafarer he'd met at the museum and responded accordingly.

"Firstly, there's the possibility of collision with another vessel—common enough in naval history. Furthermore, the North Atlantic at this time of the year is plagued by massive icebergs that have broken away from the main ice-flow. Imagine what's likely to happen if the Titanic hits one of those things at twenty knots or more knowing she's carrying insufficient lifeboats to cover a major contingency."

At this point, the chief surveyor gave thought for the first time as to what he was being asked to do and the responsibility he was undertaking in signing the safety certificate which, although strictly within the law, morally left much to worry about in the light of what his young assistant had said. The concerned look that now appeared on his face told his assistant his comments had hit home.

"Even if I believe there is a genuine concern in this matter, what are you suggesting we do?"

The young man felt a little surprised that his superior should be asking him what the next steps should be.

"I'm not sure, Sir, but isn't there a method of appeal enabling us to raise our observations so that, at least, we'd have it on record that we raised the issue and gave our views should anything occur? I know it's a million to one against, and Titanic will almost certainly have a successful and trouble-free voyage but..." he looked pleadingly at his superior, "...just in case, don't you think?"

By this time conscience had intervened and was starting to overcome legal practicality in the mind of the chief surveyor. In addition, he was inwardly anxious that his own position was safely covered as well.

"The only person I can approach is Captain Harvey Clark, the Board of Trade Inspector. Anything higher would have to come through him."

"Well, then Sir, could I suggest you contact him and at least put our request on record."

It was several days later and less than a week before Titanic was due to set off on her maiden voyage when a group of important and serious looking men assembled at the offices of the White Star Line close to Southampton docks where Titanic was currently taking on crew and provisions. Those present in respect of the White Star Line included Bruce Ismay, its managing director, Lord James Pirie, director of Harland and Wolff, the Belfast shipbuilders who built the Titanic, Thomas Andrews who actually supervised the building of the ship and Captain Edward James Smith, the ship's captain who had recently brought her from Belfast Lough to her current berth in Southampton docks. Those on the other side having called the meeting were Francis Carruthers, Board of Trade surveyor along with his young assistant who we have already met. Despite the fact that this was neither a court of law nor an official inquiry, the meeting was to be presided over, as agreed to by both parties, by Sir John Charles Bigham, a high court judge and often referred to as Lord Mersey. Sitting at the head of a long table with the two parties sitting opposite each other, it was he who opened the proceedings.

"This meeting has been called by the Board of Trade, represented today by Francis Carruthers, the Board's chief surveyor. As you are all probably aware by now, the reason for the meeting is to consider some safety matters that Mr

Carruthers felt should be discussed before the Titanic commences her maiden voyage next week. I further mention that while this meeting has no legal validity to enforce matters, I trust the issue will be debated and ultimately decided by mutual agreement. On that basis, I call upon Mr Carruthers to state the matter to be debated."

Carruthers cleared his throat before putting his observations before the august gathering of White Star officials opposite.

"When the Titanic leaves Southampton next Wednesday, 10 April 1912 on her maiden voyage, she will have on board a total of some 2,229 passengers and crew. As things stand at present, she will carry 20 lifeboats of one kind or another, Fourteen fully fledged boats can carry 65 people each, two emergency cutters will hold 40 people each and four collapsible lifeboats will take 47 people each. If fully and properly loaded, that is a total of 1,178 people capable of being transferred to lifeboats in case of an emergency. It will not have escaped your attention, gentlemen, that it would leave 1,051 souls still on board and, in the case of a disaster, likely to lose their lives. The Board of Trade, on whose behalf I myself will sign the certificate of safety and seaworthiness do, therefore, strongly recommend that the complement of lifeboats be increased from 20 to 40 which would safely cater for all passengers and crew due to be carried on this voyage."

At this point Justice Bigham addressed the meeting.

"Mr Carruthers has explained and put the proposition to the meeting. Assuming all understand clearly what has been proposed, I call on the White Star Company and its representatives to respond."

The first to reply was the White Star's managing director Bruce Ismay.

"I note your observations, Mr Carruthers, but you must know that the lifeboat complement is, in fact, well within the maritime law as presently constituted."

"Yes, it is, Mr Ismay, but that is due to the fact, as we all know, that maritime engineering moves much faster than maritime law. However, I would suggest that the moral imperative in this case clearly outweighs the legal one surely. Are we really saying that it is acceptable in principle to allow this great liner to set sail on its maiden voyage with almost half its passengers and crew potentially in danger?"

"But Mr Carruthers, we're talking about a 46,329-ton seagoing leviathan; the ship's unsinkable, Sir!"

"Oh no, she isn't, Mr Ismay! No ship is unsinkable. The Titanic is made of iron and steel; should she be holed below the waterline, she'll sink alright, as sure as night follows day."

Seemingly defeated, Ismay went quiet, but Thomas Andrews the Titanic's builder intervened.

"Assuming the unlikely event you outline, Mr Carruthers, we have installed six large bulkheads that would protect the ship from inundation."

Carruther's response was instant and telling.

"You of all people, Mr Andrews, should know that the bulkheads though large and impressive as you claim do not reach up to the deck above. This means that once flooded the water would overlap the first bulkhead then into the next and so on so that before long the ship's bow would start to sink below the surface."

It was now the engineer's turn to lapse into silence having had his defence of the ship's safety undermined. In a desperate attempt to redress the situation, Lord James Pirie the White Star director intervened sharply.

"But what in God's name is going to sink such a massive ship even if we accept your assessment of its ultimate vulnerability?"

At this point, before replying, Carruthers glanced at his young assistant sitting beside him and smiled knowing that what he was about to say came from him.

"Lord Pirie, our maritime history books are full of accounts of ships colliding in the most unusual circumstances, in addition to which it is not unknown for large ships to hit underwater obstructions such as rocks. But there is another danger, remote it must be said, but one that lurks nevertheless. Next Wednesday, 10 April, Titanic will leave Southampton and make her way to Cherbourg for a short stay. Thereafter she will sail to the west coast of Ireland making a last call at Queenstown before setting course for New York and the North Atlantic. The likelihood...no, the almost certainty is that your wonderful vessel will have a pleasant and uninterrupted journey arriving at her destination within the week. However, it so happens at this time of year that the slightly warmer spring weather starts to melt the ice in the northern pole. This leads to massive icebergs breaking away from the main ice-flow and drifting southwards. If visibility is poor, it just may happen that Titanic may inadvertently hit one of these massive floating obstructions. In such an event have you any idea what is likely to happen to your ship?"

In an effort to redeem himself, Thomas Andrews intervened confidently.

"Even should such an unlikely event occur, the ship would shudder to a stop with some internal discomfort to passengers, but she would certainly not sink."

"Quite so, Mr Andrews, assuming she hit the berg head on. But what if the iceberg hit the ship's side gouging a massive hole below the water line while hundreds of rivets pop out like chestnuts from a brazier and seawater starts rushing in? Soon the lower decks would be flooded and, as we've just seen, water would quickly overflow the bulwarks with the certain and fatal consequence that the Titanic would eventually sink."

This final put-down along with such a dreadful interpretation of the consequences seemed to stun the ship owner's representatives. They remained silent trying to absorb the apocalyptic possibility of their ship's demise as outlined by the Board of Trade's chief surveyor. Carruthers seized the moment and completed his summing up.

"As I have conceded all along, the possibility of such a dreadful happening is remote. However, it is surely the responsibility of you as owners to cover all contingencies when dealing with the lives of so many people. I assume you have taken out adequate insurance to cover the ship in all such contingencies. But that insurance, gentlemen, will not cover the passengers and crew should such a disaster strike. Their insurance surely lies in the adequacy of the number of lifeboats that are available and that will ensure that they and their families can be safely carried to safety. On that note, gentlemen, I rest my case and merely reiterate the request I made at the outset of this meeting. Increase the number of lifeboats on the Titanic from 20 to 40 so that from next Wednesday onwards we ourselves may sleep peacefully in our beds knowing that everything possible has been done to ensure the safety of 2,229 passengers and crew on board as your magnificent ship sets out on its momentous maiden voyage. Thank you."

Sensing matters had concluded Justice Bigham brought the meeting to a close.

"May I suggest the members of White Star adjourn to discuss the matter before letting us know their reaction? I suggest we reconvene here in one hour."

It was Tuesday, 16 April 1912, when the young man sat at his breakfast table at home, the morning newspaper propped up on the table in front of him. He, and the rest of the world, had already learned the previous day what happened to the Titanic, but because it had occurred in the early hours of Monday morning, today was the first occasion since the disaster that the morning papers could print the story. The headline was dramatic:

"TITANIC SINKS AFTER COLLISION WITH ICEBERG!"

However, it was the sub-heading that took the young man's eye:

"No fatalities as all passengers and crew are safely rescued."

He smiled to himself as he read the accompanying account of what occurred. It seems that the ship struck the iceberg at 11:40 pm on the evening of Sunday, 14 April, eventually sinking at 2:20 am on Monday, 15 April. In the intervening period, thanks to the discipline and efficiency of the Captain Edward Smith and his officers, Murdoch and Lightoller in particular, all passengers and crew members were safely guided on to the forty or so lifeboats that the White Star line had, in their wisdom, provided. The account went on to say that after some four hours drifting in the cold waters of the North Atlantic, they were rescued by the SS Carpathia and another vessel that picked up the SOS signals. It was expected that the vessels would dock in New York at Cunard's pier 54 sometime on 18 April when a large crowd of welcoming and relieved observers would be present. The article concluded by saying that while the loss of such a magnificent ship as the Titanic was, in itself, a disaster, the fact that all on board were saved can only be a matter of great relief and also a recognition of the great foresight of the White Star company whose diligent provision of sufficient lifeboats prevented what would have almost certainly been a huge human tragedy.

The young man slowly folded the paper and pushed it to one side, drained his teacup before picking up his coat from a nearby chair and, after shouting goodbye to his mother in the kitchen, opened the front door and strode out into the chill morning air.